Marki's eyebrows rose in surprise and pleasure. Without a heartbeat's hesitation she grasped Tru by the shoulders and with slow certainty turned Tru away from the mirrored wall and into a comforting embrace.

Tru watched the crowded dance floor as Marki's hands swept over her. One hand slid inside her jacket and under the quickly unbuttoned shirt to caress her breasts. In the darkness under the wide sheltering edge of the mahogany bar, Marki's other hand moved firmly down the front of Tru's jeans and stroked through the seamed denim. The touch seared Tru's flesh.

Tru's breath caught in her throat, and a liquefying fire spread through her where Marki's hands roamed. The heat swelled up from Tru's crotch and spread across her breasts.

"I don't think..." Tru struggled to clear her throat and move away from the imploring hand.

"Sometimes it's best not to," Marki throatily suggested, pulling Tru closer. Tru's struggles for escape slowed and changed to a thrust against Marki's resourceful hand.

A TRU NORTH MYSTERY 1

KC Bomber

Janet McClellan

THE NAIAD PRESS, INC.
1997

Printed in the United States of America on acid-free paper
First Edition

Editor: Lila Empson
Cover designer: Bonnie Liss (Phoenix Graphics)
Typesetter: Sandi Stancil

Library of Congress Cataloging-in-Publication Data

McClellan, Janet, 1951 –
 K.C. Bomber : a Tru North mystery / Janet McClellan.
  p.   cm.
 ISBN 1-56280-157-0 (p)
 1. Lesbians—Fiction. I. Title.
PS3563.C3413K2   1997
813'.54—dc21
                                                    96-45484
                                                       CIP

In loving memory, to Dad,
who delighted and worried
through the adventures and exploits
of my career in law enforcement
(and my life in general).
Wish you were here to share with.

Acknowledgments

To all the folks at and working with Naiad for patience, guidance, and all their hard work.

About the Author

Janet E. McClellan began her career in law enforcement at the tender age of nineteen. She has worked twenty-six years for various criminal justice agencies as a patrol officer, undercover investigator, detective, college professor, and prison/correction systems manager. At forty-five she has returned to law enforcement and is the Police Chief in a small town in Kansas.

Chapter 1

The distant trains moaned through the frosty night air as they bore down on the faintly protesting steel rails. Their cries moved out and away from the city. Forces beyond the control of wheels and tracks moved the trains past each other toward their separate destinations. Darkness nestled close to the waters of the river below.

A woman stood on the bridge above the railroad yard and imagined the trains gripping their hot bellies as they moved through the night. The sounds of steel calling to steel receded. Their pounding withdrawal eased the reverberations under her feet and left her to a dark misery. Their sounds mimicked her restlessness, and her sad laughter followed the trains speeding out to the wide flat prairie.

The moments passed, and she was left with the fears she muzzled in the raised fleece collar of her jacket. She was lost in the half-death feeling that her life had become.

She flicked her last cigarette over the railing of the bridge, leaned over, and watched the small red glare wink out as it fell into the cold water below.

She felt as though her mind had shut down. She had felt like that for weeks. Her eyes followed the miniature whirlpools conjured in the deep river and smashed against the jetties. Churning waters danced before her while the muted fluorescent lights of the bridge cast their dim reflection on the surface beneath her. The swirling called to her, hypnotizing her to come join the last dance. She leaned daringly over the railing to watch the circling pools. How far could they dance? Would they join other pools in secret under the bridge and be together in one brief moment? Did they increase themselves or lose everything within a jumble of torrents?

Stepping up and onto a cross beam, she balanced her curiosity against caution and wavered on the edge of the wide iron rail. She eased herself against the bracing and lay down on the I-beam. Her head rested on her right arm, her left hand gripping the rail as she embraced an imaginary cold lover. Her right leg dangled back toward the forgotten safe purchase as the other leg rested uneasily on the riveted joining.

She fought down a mounting melancholy. In spite of the fear, her body lay still against the iron while her face drew itself up into questioning poses, frowns, and complaints.

The metal's chilled surface bit slowly through her jacket, the light blue shirt beneath, and along the blue-jeaned length of her body. The chill found her warm flesh and stroked it with icy fingers. It spread across her breasts and down her belly. The power of the cold in the iron battled against her lassitude. Slow frigid fingers urged her away from her precarious perch.

Raising herself on her arms, she tucked a leg beneath her, arched her back, thrust her body forward, and jumped away from the beam. An instant later, Tru North's booted feet jarred heavily against the solid safety of the bridge.

Chapter 2

The twenty-minute drive back into the city was accompanied with the car's heat vents pouring full blast over Tru's chilled and shivering body. The heated blasts could not replenish her warmth or soften her mood. Kansas City, Missouri, was still chilled by a reluctant and tenacious winter in mid-March. The persistent spring rains had prolonged the frosty nights, lacing them with a cool moisture-laden thickness. Tru's emotional state matched the weather conditions of the last three weeks. The gray haze of winter lingered in her shrinking soul as easily as the clouded skies hugged the spires of downtown buildings.

Drawn by a need and desire she would not name, she drove to a half-forgotten haunt. Tru parked the car in the shadows of the building, left the engine running, and waited outside the bar. The touch of the cold iron that clung to her chest and groin sent sharp shivers up and down her frame. Looking at the glaring announcement of the bar's neon sign, she knew she did not want to go inside. But she refused to go back to an empty apartment. She was reluctant to make any decision beyond her own thin awareness of not daring to be alone with her thoughts. After the bridge, she no longer trusted herself to her own good care. Caught between place and time, she could not be certain she could trust herself with others. As she sat in her car she could hear the sounds of music that flashed and blasted toward her as the heavy double doors opened and closed.

Women of all shapes and sizes, smiling and laughing, touching, arms clasping one another, came and went through the doors. She watched them and envied them from the darkness of her car. She was a stranger to their contentment and estranged from the vitality of their moods.

"Courage," she called softly to herself. "How bad could it be?" Plenty, the tiny voice in her head chided. She had met Eleanor at the bar three years ago. Going in now would be an act of hopelessness or worse. A resignation. A disillusioned romantic longing for the past. Tru felt repulsed by the memory of broken promises, misplaced trust, and shattered dreams. The bar was the last place she wanted to be and the first place she needed to go.

The last time she had been in the bar was over six months ago. A lifetime. She had been with Eleanor, and they had shared that which had passed for love, caring, and trust. It would not be the same. Eleanor was gone, and because of it Tru knew she was as different and wounded as Eleanor had intended. Mocking laughter still echoed in Tru's ears long after Eleanor had left her for someone else. It had numbed Tru for weeks. The basic and mechanical routines of life were all she'd been able to muster until tonight.

"Just one drink for warmth, crowded companionship," she coaxed herself. "And then home to bed, alone," she promised quietly, hoping she might hear the sound of conviction.

Tru took a deep breath and swung open the car door. Summoning what little courage she had left, she walked across the parking lot and through the beckoning doors. Tru North squared her shoulders and strode into the vibrant lights with the back beat of rock 'n' roll calling to her.

"Sally forth, sally on, Sally Ride, ride, Sally ride," Tru chanted to herself in mock encouragement.

Walking through the narrow entrance, her body was assaulted by the sounds, smells, and undulating lights of a Friday night desperate-to-dance bar scene. Her head reeled. Bodies moved through the vacillating lights and sweeping darkness of the room. Through the piercing strobe-light oscillations, she briefly recalled the magnetic spell of the river and quickly wished it away. Here, inside the bar, the rhythmic movement and tempo pulled and tempted her toward life. The distant river had been much more menacing.

A voice close to her suddenly urged her renewed attentiveness to the present.

"Two bucks cover and identification, please." The woman who spoke to Tru sat at the entrance, resting easily on a tall bar stool. She was dressed in all the appropriate bouncer regalia of black jeans, boots, jean jacket, and silky white shirt. Her hair was pulled back into a short, loose auburn ponytail. She was tall, and if she decided to stand Tru knew the woman would tower over her by more than a head. Tru observed that the woman was pleasingly well formed. Solid and not an ounce of fat on the lounging frame. She looked formidable, but her otherwise severe impression disappeared as she smiled. Grinning broadly at Tru's silent blinking question, the woman repeated her request.

"Two bucks and your ID. I need to see if you're old enough to be in here." Straight white teeth flashed a fetching grin.

Tru nodded obliquely and reached into her right hip pocket for her wallet. She carefully palmed her gold badge and handed two ones to the woman. Tonight the bar was for pleasure, not business. Tru retrieved her driver's license from beneath the police department identification card and held the license up for the woman's inspection.

The bouncer looked at the license and back into Tru's face. A smaller half-smile came over her lips.

"Tru North? Now, is that really your name?" The woman's dark hazel eyes reflected the sparkle of the dance-floor strobe.

"Yes, for more than thirty-four years," Tru sighed in response. She was used to the questions about her name but was too tired and distracted to respond with her usual light banter. This was not the time for telling personal or family stories. Forgetfulness was her real friend tonight, and Tru wanted to find it somewhere in the darkness. Tru wanted to get through the entrance, seat herself at the bar, have the one drink she had promised herself, and be gone.

"Nice to have you here," the bouncer said, returning the license as her eyes slid slowly over Tru.

Tru felt more than saw the woman's eyes. She allowed the scrutiny and felt assured in her attractiveness. She was small but knew she was in proportion to her height, weight, and small bone structure. Her frequent and habitual workouts at the gym had given Tru tight muscles and a dancer's poise. Mid-length brown hair and large gray eyes softened Tru's look as much as it belied her practiced strength. Tru felt herself straighten a little under the other's steady gaze. Unconsciously, she asserted herself up to her full five feet five inches of height and dared the other woman to look away. But Tru lost the scrutiny contest as unbidden memories pulled her eyes toward the interior of the Round Table Bar, her once old and now new again home away from home.

The Round Table was cleaner and neater than she had remembered. It had finally vanquished the brassy posters and declarations of the trivial drug-culture pretensions of an earlier generation. The new owners had transformed the bar from an aborted modernistic design to a hardworking decor of ice-on-pastel chrome furniture, slightly padded chairs, and short industrial-nap carpet that covered all but the polished dance floor.

It was a women's bar. And for the first time in Tru's memory it finally looked like it had something other than the traditional ambience of a flea market.

Because it was a women's club, the number of customers was small most nights of the week. When the crowds were larger, as now, the bar would be filled with the young, the older, the bevies of friends, the restless seekers and the predatorially eager. It was not necessarily a bar that would be relished by Tru's politically reformed, upwardly mobile, and professionally secured sisters. But even that fact did not keep the well-heeled and the working-class moderates from drifting in and out of the bar and one another's lives.

The Round Table was a bar where the edges and separate patterns of lesbian lifestyles were quilted together. The style, fabrics, callings, and chance meetings were inclusive and diverse in a manner the straight world illiterately called "alternative lifestyles." *Lifestyle* had more than one definition. The bar was a lively microcosm of proof that how one lived was a matter of nurture and nature, choice and chance. And the chance for choices in nature was unlimited.

Straight women occasionally wandered in and stared deer-dumb at a world they denied and rejected while they pursued their sheepskins and MRS. degrees or hid in their protective corporate coloration. Their aura set them off from the regulars and screened them from the lives they had stumbled upon. They were rarely bothered and, if approached, it was usually on a dare from a table of mildly intoxicated revelers seeking a diversion.

Older coupled women, aged fifty-five and beyond, would sometimes wander in to take a table and stay for a drink or two. They would just as quickly leave and go back to their condos, stylish walk-ups, and other settled middle-class comforts.

The regulars, the ones who had partnered, unpartnered, played and lost to drift again, made up the majority of any night's crowd. These women of like minds held forth against a sea of longing. Their longing ranged from romance to simple hot-eyed desire. The bar was a refuge where women could hold hands and hold each other without prying, judgmental eyes attacking who they were. The bar was a walled city, set away from the other metropolis, happy in its existence and the companions it assembled to itself. Tru was home again and mostly glad of it.

Tru experienced some difficulty retrieving her license as the other woman's fingers held hers and lingered lightly for a moment longer than seemed absolutely necessary. Tru pocketed the laminated card and nodded to the bouncer without acknowledging either the touch or the possibility of the message in the fingertips.

Despite newer decorations and a general sense of freshness in the surroundings, things had not changed much at the bar. Tru wondered if old standbys like having a bouncer in black were requisite to women's-bar training programs. Tru had learned early on in her alternative career that most of the bouncers in women's clubs were notorious flirts. The one she had encountered at the door appeared to have subscribed to the typecasting. As she let the music draw her away from the club's entrance, Tru chuckled at the thought that no matter how things or time changed, much seemed to stay the same.

Propelling herself forward through an uneven sea of bodies, Tru wondered how long it would take to make her way to the bar's brass railing. Halfway across the floor, as the crowd surged against her, she felt the rise of misgivings wash over her. She was reluctant to move forward. The crowd shifted and surged as an animal stretching its muscles, reflexes, and claws. The movement brought back Tru's recessed aversions to too many people and too much noise in one place.

Of all that Tru liked about being surrounded by women, this combination of battling bodies, oppressive conversational cacophony, smoke, and ear-shattering music had never been among them. She did not want to retreat but did not know how she could move forward through the squash of bodies that jostled around her. The drink she had wanted seemed less likely now than it had when she had been on the bridge railing. Chastising herself, she marveled at her foolishness and speculated about a simple, hasty, and self-preserving retreat.

Overwhelmed, Tru hesitated at the sturdy iron fence surrounding the pool tables. She leaned on the low structure that separated the crowd from the players. Tru's right hand sought her throbbing temples, and she tried to rub away a newly acquired ache. She slumped for several moments to rethink her purpose and get the bearings on her expanding distress. Lassitude washed over her. She leaned in to the fence, recalling giddily that she had not eaten during the last two days. Her hunger and the disquiet evoked by the crowd weakened her knees.

"You okay, honey?" A supporting hand and arm slid across her shoulders, gently tucking her into a firm grip.

Tru looked up uncertainly into the face of the woman who held her in an uncompromising embrace. The cerebral fog that had settled tenaciously over her momentarily hid the other's identity. Mystified and relieved, Tru tried to remember who the woman was and where she had come from.

"You okay?" the voice repeated softly as it filtered its way through the music's pulsing beat and into Tru's head.

"Yes, I am . . . I'm just tired," Tru muttered self-consciously as she recognized the club's bouncer. Tru straightened her shoulders to gain release from the woman's hold. Breathing deeply in what she hoped was a self-contained assertion, Tru turned her face away from the warm supporting arms to signal her intention to move away.

The bouncer moved her hand, letting it slide down Tru's shoulder and across her back, patting and rubbing as it went. The touch vanished without further suggestive exploration. The woman's eyes never wavered from Tru's face.

"You don't look or act as if you're an ordinary kind of tired to me. I'll keep an eye on you just the same."

"Fine, suit yourself," Tru said, knowing her voice sounded too sharp. Her irritation at herself came spilling out and flowed over the other woman. Hastily trying to muster what few manners she could remember Tru affirmed, "It has been . . . it's been a rough week. I am not much like myself. Thanks anyway."

Tru steadied herself and tried to move out into the crowd again but was stalled by a lingering hand holding her to the spot. Leaning close to Tru's ear, the bouncer's arm encircled her shoulders. She whispered resonantly, "Make no mistake. I mean no harm. You look lost and a little in need. Part's my job, mostly it's interest," she said, releasing Tru.

"Thank you . . ."

"Marki," the woman offered.

"Thank you, Marki. I think I'll find that drink I was looking for when I came in."

"By the way," Marki raised her voice and let it follow Tru across the floor. "If you're not 'much like' yourself tonight, who do you think you're like, and . . . would I like her?"

Tru glanced back and shrugged a gentle answering dismissal in Marki's direction. It was all she dared to do. Tru had noticed that Bouncer Marki had lovely eyes and a solid warm feel, neither of which Tru wanted anything to do with. Tru felt cold and distant from the world. The feeling had surrounded her for so many weeks that she knew she was no longer a good judge of either kindness or intentions. She was not up to dealing with that woman's potential persistent generosity. Tru knew she was no match for anything or anyone more charming than a frosted mug of beer. She had her pride, and precious little of that, since Eleanor.

"Goddess," Tru exclaimed, as she waged bodily

war toward a bar stool. As she finally sat down, the woman on the next bar stool glanced at her with a raised eyebrow.

"Muttering to myself," she offered to the other's unvoiced question. Quickly turning her attention to the matter at hand, Tru caught the eye of a harried bartender and signaled for a bourbon and draft beer back.

While she waited, the thought of Eleanor flashed across her mind, and her heart vibrated in instant discord in her chest. Wryly, she wondered why some stranger would find her more interesting than her own lost Eleanor had. Perversity. It was the sheer perversity of possibilities, Tru acknowledged hopelessly as the first bourbon and chaser arrived.

She drank steadily at her own pace, and the night wore on. Shortly before midnight the crowd began to thin. Tru gratefully recalled that she was off duty the next two days and could afford to indulge in a third bourbon and beer. The last two had let her slip away through time without doing any harm to herself other than that her butt was getting a little tired of holding itself on the perch. As she leaned against the bar, Tru shifted for comfort. Aching buns were a minor inconvenience to the alternative of going home.

She felt lucky. She'd found a safe corner at the back edge of the dark counter and had successfully stalled advances from cruising women. Tru imagined a barrier of stone and ice between her and the room. She had lowered the barrier twice and then only long enough to signal the bartender for another round.

Her brooding countenance worked like a charm or a curse. Either way, she knew it was best not to seek company regardless of how desperate she felt the need. She did not want to harm herself, the misguided, or the innocent through some miscalculated communication. She kept everyone at a firm distance. She wasn't fit company, that's what Eleanor had said, and the thought made her eyes smart and mist in memory.

Tru chuckled ruefully into her drink. A mute agony intruded on her fog; barricading herself against feeling was no major accomplishment. She'd done it before. She'd driven Eleanor away, or let her go, or something equally final and devastating. Tru knew her barriers weren't hard to manufacture. She knew she carried a wall, high, firm, and sure. It had become her life's story. The barrier had always been easy to assemble and was available in a moment's notice. It arose at the first sign of fear or hint of discontent. It was, she bitterly acknowledged, unassailable by logic or compromise to any regrets but her own. And tonight, not even to those.

Shaking her head, Tru told herself that it had not always been that way. It hadn't even begun that way with Eleanor. Eleanor had been so very angry with the world and, because of her availability, angrier at Tru. In the time they had been together, they had parted frequently, realigned their uncertainties, and joined again. Not this time. This time, there was no going back, no counter to the anger, and no hope for recovery.

The anger and separateness that had been Eleanor's life had insinuated itself into Tru's and finally had ruled them both. Eleanor's anger at the world, herself, people in general, and men in particular had turned her into an overcontrolling, jealous, and demanding shrew. Eleanor's need to dominate

Tru's every waking moment suffocated their relationship. The control had grown slowly until Tru was certain it would crush her. She had fought to set herself free before it consumed her. Fearful it would eat her alive as surely as separatist fury had consumed Eleanor, Tru shrank away from that withering touch and began to psychologically leave Eleanor in order to save herself.

Eleanor sensed her going and raced her to the finish. But on her way out, Eleanor had managed to punish Tru one final time. It was a calculated indignity planned for a night she had worked late. Tru had opened the bedroom door to find Eleanor locked in erotic embrace with another woman. Eleanor's ultimate ridicule was to berate Tru for her lack of passion and commitment in their relationship as Eleanor lay in their bed holding the other woman. Tru stood in the doorway numb and dumbfounded at the brazen tableau while the other woman laughed.

Tru left the house unable to make any more futile excuses for Eleanor or herself. Tru fled the house just before she lost what little control remained and used the 9mm slung under her shoulder. The blinding shock and half-paralysis of the encounter had been a blessing. Otherwise she would have been facing murder charges instead of a night's glass of beer.

The third bourbon and beer had drowned out the questions and mental protests regarding her decision to stay at the bar. Ordering again, Tru wondered if a fourth bourbon and beer would wash away the lingering vision of the railroad bridge and her flirtation with the final darkness.

I couldn't have really done that. I wasn't thinking about it, Tru argued silently with herself. Just tired. Water's soothing. It was hypnotizing me . . . making me feel calmer, that's all. Mesmerized by waves and self-inflicted pain. Simple. No point in going back when nothing's there; no point in going forward when you don't know where to go.

The alcohol let her mind play tag with her misery, circling on itself, arguing in and out of despair.

"Stupid," Tru said, struggling to sit up a little straighter and taller on the stool. Here's fun, she thought, muttering haplessly at the bottom of her fourth glass. Abruptly losing her balance, she partially slid off the stool, caught herself, and wavered uncertainly at the bar rail.

"It's only stupid if you have another," Marki said as she moved onto the bar stool and sat behind Tru. As Marki sat down, she parted her knees and let her legs encircle Tru. The press of her thighs moved lightly against Tru's hips.

The undemanding yet immediate pressure obliged Tru to turn and face the woman. Marki smiled in pleasure and mocked innocent alarm at Tru.

"I'll give you to the count of three to stop that," Tru said, surprised at her own tone. Her flirtation fluttered against her inebriated conscience, and she locked caution in a little room at the back of her mind.

"Ninety-nine, ninety-eight, ninety-seven . . ." Tru dared Marki through the bourbon.

Marki's eyebrows rose in surprise and pleasure. Without a heartbeat's hesitation she grasped Tru by the shoulders and with slow certainty turned Tru away from the mirrored wall and into a comforting embrace.

Tru watched the crowded dance floor as Marki's hands swept over her. One hand slid inside her jacket and under the quickly unbuttoned shirt to caress her breasts. In the darkness under the wide sheltering edge of the mahogany bar, Marki's other hand moved firmly down the front of Tru's jeans and stroked through the seamed denim. The touch seared Tru's flesh.

Tru's breath caught in her throat, and a liquefying fire spread through her where Marki's hands roamed. The heat swelled up from Tru's crotch and spread across her breasts.

"I don't think..." Tru struggled to clear her throat and move away from the imploring hand.

"Sometimes it's best not to," Marki throatily suggested, pulling Tru closer. Tru's struggles for escape slowed and changed to a thrust against Marki's resourceful hand.

The noise in the bar rained down on them as they quietly moved in mutual embrace. Tru's desire increased. She was awash with yearning, and the months of torturous dalliance with Eleanor became fuel for the fire in Tru's body.

Tru gasped and sucked air between her teeth, her longings and aches rising within her.

Some mental perversity let Eleanor's features float up to her mind's eye again. Eleanor had not touched her for months and had not touched her lovingly for a long time before that. Eleanor had wanted Tru to be a blank slate to Eleanor's desire and minor mental cruelties. She had left Tru more than a little shattered and uncertain as to whether or not she was interesting, attractive, or even capable of being touched by anyone. But Tru was being touched now.

Marki's hands moved to silently answer Tru's unspoken desire and to feed the craving intensity of her need.

The music stopped, and the crowd surged closer along the wide edges of the bar. The crush of bodies distracted by alcohol were oblivious to the capering between Tru and Marki. Little tight circles of friends, acquaintances, and strangers were entertaining themselves in their own merriment, unaware of the shadowed compromise at the remote corner of the bar.

Tru felt herself swooning and closed her eyes in acquiescence to the firmness of Marki's hand. Tru opened her eyes and looked around uncertainly. She wondered if she were trapped in a misty dream or if what she was experiencing was an incredible reality. Her consuming desire and the sudden awareness of potential public display mixed wildly and excitedly within her.

Marki rubbed and kneaded the soft flesh between Tru's legs and pulled her forefinger firmly across the wetness seeping through her denim. Marki moved her full hand down Tru's crotch and palmed her. Her hand roughly glided up as she let her two middle fingers wriggle in slow suggestion against Tru's heat-seeking vulva. A throaty gurgling rose from Tru's throat.

"Darlin', someone been starving you at home?" Marki crooned into Tru's ear.

"Hmm," was all that Tru could muster.

"Doesn't your lady know anything . . . anything

about you, what you need, what you like, or want?"
Marki's throatily whispered questions stabbed deep
into Tru's troubled heart.

Lost to the heat and spreading warmth in her
groin, Tru did not feel the unsnapping of the first
three buttons on her 501's. She did feel Marki's hand
slide unhesitatingly into her jeans, down past her
panties, teasing at her hairline and lingering on the
edge of her mons veneris.

Panicking, Tru wanted to stop Marki, but then
she meltingly relented, not wanting her to stop, ever.
Tru was being touched in public and being driven
crazy with a longing she didn't want to control.
Moaning softly, Tru leaned back into Marki's breasts
and averted her eyes from the blurring faces of the
crowd. Accepting the request and acknowledging the
surrender, Marki's strong fingers urgently pushed
between the lips of Tru's vulva and expertly trapped
her clitoris between her fingers. Marki held her hand
in the soft wet embrace of Tru's quivering lips and
let the tip of her index finger tease at the flooding
vestibule.

Tru felt as though she were fainting as Marki
raised her ever so slightly off the floor with a strong
left arm and helped herself to bold access of Tru's
lavish need. Marki hesitated slightly; she stroked and
waited knowingly for the involuntary gasp to which
the quivering flesh would succumb. Under the
ministrations of her teasingly tormenting finger, Tru's
vagina quivered and opened to her. Marki bedeviled
Tru for one delightful moment longer to eliminate
hesitation or vacillation in the need consuming Tru.
She smoothly thrust her finger inside.

Tru arched and surged in Marki's hand. Her

thrusting hip gave the opportunity, and Marki moved her hand to markedly deepen the thrust to two fingers as she pushed the snug jeans material away from Tru's crotch. Marki's hand nudged against the fabric and pulled open a space to give her access for maneuvering. Tru fumbled with her jacket, stripped it off, and lay it across her lap as a last fragile vestige of propriety to help her from exposing herself in the dark of the bar. Taking advantage of the cover Tru provided, Marki pulled Tru farther up on her lap and let the rub of material push Tru's jeans down her thighs. Under the jacket Tru's nakedness and openness to Marki left them gasping in a mutual wildfire.

Tru let it happen. She wanted to feel everything. She wanted it to feel right, deep, and right now. She sank into a delirium of the motions of Marki's hand. Succumbing to her own submerged yearning, she forgot the world outside her hunger.

Opening her eyes, Tru saw the bartender staring at her. The woman looked directly into her eyes. She understood everything and knew what Tru was feeling the instant their eyes met. Their eyes stayed locked on each other until Marki groaned hungrily into Tru's ear. The bartender looked past Tru to Marki. For a moment, she stared wide-eyed at Marki. Slowly, the bartender turned and walked to the other end of the bar and tried to look busy as she absently dried a glass in her hand. Tru closed her eyes and became lost to everything but Marki's sweet solicitations.

"I, I can't . . ." Tru faintly struggled.

"Oh, but you can," crooned Marki, "and you're just about to. Aren't you?" Marki urged.

Tru wanted to fight her way from the insistent fingers, and she moved in turmoil against Marki's embrace. But her efforts to disengage herself from Marki merely helped to tantalize her traitorous clitoris.

Having narrowly escaped a death wish earlier in the evening, Tru knew that now another and sweeter petite mort swelled inside her. Somewhere near her center and down to her toes, a force was rising to consume her. She swayed, tightening her throat to keep silent the screaming physical release that tore at her. It propelled her back against Marki, who held on to her with firm, sure arms.

Marki let the moment take Tru. She urged Tru down shuddering roads of unabashed craving and through layers of sweet delivery. Marki held Tru as they rode out the coursing torrents. Tru rocked and bucked in constrained submission to the orgasmic storm. Marki's hand demanded more, her fingers persisted in rallying climactic wave after wave until Tru wavered on the edge of orgasmic overload. Tru was coming and coming again at the slightest movement of Marki's submerged fingers.

Exhaustion collapsed Tru back into Marki's supporting arms. Tru's vagina sucked spasmodically around Marki's tauntingly submerged fingers.

Tru held on to Marki's thighs for support as her knees deserted her and welcomed the solid embrace she found again in Marki's arms. Long moments passed before Tru was capable of regaining any semblance of her earlier composure. Her chest still heaving from the strain, Tru feebly tried to find the buttons on her jeans. She fumbled ineffectively with leaden fingers and in defeat let her hands fall helplessly to her sides.

Marki slowly pulled her hand away from Tru's traumatized clitoris and reached down, pulled up, and helped to refasten Tru's jeans. Tenderly hugging Tru to her breasts, Marki gently rocked Tru and whispered soft murmuring sounds of satisfaction in her ear.

Tru felt her eyes begin to brim as ragged breaths filled her lungs. Marki's soft muttering only intensified Tru's rising distress.

"I'd like you to come home with me," Marki whispered. "Some holding, some being. No harm, demands, or risks," Marki soothed. Tru's ragged breathing stilled Marki's voice.

Tru looked wildly about. She wanted to escape from her self-anger and astonished shame.

"It seems to me you need a lot of TLC, darlin'. Somebody's not treating you right," Marki persisted.

"I need to . . . I need to go to the bathroom." Tru struggled and swallowed hard against the salty tears in her throat. Remorse and anxiety swept through her. Her mind was a sudden torrent of recrimination and confusion. She no longer knew who she was, what she was, or what she was doing. She only knew she wanted to get away.

"All right," Marki said, releasing her tender hold. "I'll be waiting." She kissed Tru softly on the temple and watched in delight and buoyant fascination as Tru made her unsteady way across the long room toward the bathroom doors.

Tru tried to steady herself on her teetering legs. Self-pity and rancor rushed over her. She didn't know if she had used Marki, if Marki had used her, or both. She didn't care. She wanted to leave, and she did not want to face Marki again. Not now and, mercifully, not ever. Tru knew she was behaving cowardly. That wasn't like her, but she no longer cared. Anger flared, and she cursed at herself. She railed helplessly. But she couldn't stop herself from doing what she wanted to do, and that was to get out of the bar. To get out of the bar and as far away from Marki as possible.

Her uncertain legs managed to carry her across the room and to the bathroom hallway. She was grateful for the tune that had called so many women to dance and had cleared the hallway. Entering the bathroom, she turned back and peeked out the door in time to see Marki talking to the club manager. They left the counter and walked over to a table where three underage women were sitting. Marki had a bouncer-on-duty look about her, and Tru suspected the young women were about to be unceremoniously shown the door.

Seeing her chance, Tru took it. She dashed down the hall and without hesitation bounded through the fire escape door. Remarkably, the alarm never sounded. As she ran down the alley, Tru had a wild thought about the fine the fire marshall would levy if he knew about that piece of broken machinery.

Giggling and half-choking on sobs, Tru ran across the parking lot to her car. She climbed into the driver's seat and turned on the ignition, not daring to look back at the bar. Heading out onto the freeway, Tru promised herself that if she made it through the night she'd never go back again.

She didn't need the kind of trouble that someone like Marki would pose. Not that it would have been a big deal to Marki, Tru rationalized guiltily. Tru gave herself an excuse that Marki would quickly forget her for anything other than her surrender and that she would undoubtedly wind up simply as another notch on Marki's long list of strangers in the night. Tru snorted in self-derision. She vowed to bury the night among the other miscellaneous miscalculations of her life and go on without more twinges of guilt than her conscience would allow. Some guilt yes, but no more than what seemed to make up the rest of her life.

She knew she had to get a grip on herself, her life, her job. Her public screwing had put the fear of the goddess in her. She was becoming a wreck and knew it, knew she needed help but was unsure what kind she needed or where to get it. The one thing she did know for certain was that help wasn't going to be available through the police department shrink. He'd committed suicide last month. The poor bastard couldn't even help himself.

As she pulled in to her driveway she decided to think about it tomorrow. Even if her head wasn't clearer, it would be sober. She wanted to be free of the stupor and the misdirected desires that clouded her mind.

Tomorrow, Tru thought, tomorrow maybe she could begin to figure out where to turn or how to get her life going in the way she wanted. Maybe, she hoped, it would be easier if she ever managed to first figure out what she wanted. Pessimism and exhaustion enveloped her as she stumbled through her bedroom door, fell onto the bed, and drifted into merciful sleep.

Chapter 3

"North, get in here!" Captain Rhonn barked from the doorway of his office.

From her desk, Tru's head snapped up from the report she'd been rereading. The case was five months old. She couldn't imagine why the captain had told records to send it to her. It was intriguing and gruesome. In the report the previously assigned detective had stated that a homemade bomb, shipped through one of the local post offices, had exploded in the residence of an artist, Donald Southwick. Southwick had not survived the explosion. He had apparently been leaning over the small package, cutting the cardboard wrapping away from the enclosed wooden box, when the blast occurred. The explosive concussion in his face had fractured his skull and made soup of his brain and a mess of what had been a well-appointed office at home. The force of the sudden impact, combined with the minute slivers of wood, had created a gaping hole where most of his face had been. His body had been propelled across the room and mangled against a decorative fireplace. The scene photographs of his body made it look as though he had received the final verdict from an angry god. The blast had killed him instantly.

Before the captain had started yelling at her, Tru had decided she'd take a better look at the photographs of the crime scene later. Maybe much later and well after lunch.

Tru looked at the captain's disappearing back with unaccustomed dread. She wasn't sure what he wanted. No one ever knew what the captain wanted or from whom he wanted it. He was one of those supervisors who took delight in making career hash out of anyone who failed to guess his meanings or failed to read his mind. There was no winning with the captain at the helm, but there was no quitting for anyone who loved the work or the pension. Tru didn't know which category she belonged to. She was too young to think about a pension. She liked her work, but homicide was not something she loved. Tru's joy was in the puzzle, the chance, and the chase.

Lately, the only reason Captain Rhonn ever

wanted to talk to Tru was to reprimand her for some newly imagined impropriety. She'd become tired, distant, and vulnerable over the last few weeks, and he had been driving her harder and harder as if he knew she and Eleanor had split the sheets. No, she corrected herself, she had left Eleanor. But it didn't matter who had left whom. What did matter was that she had not been able to get a grip on herself. The weariness and dejection were becoming evident in her work. She'd started slipping in little ways and blowing things she'd once carried off without a hitch.

That was the problem. She wasn't thinking well, and sometimes it seemed to her that she wasn't thinking at all. She'd taken a hard hit at the personal level and was beginning to lose a grip on her professional conduct. Tru wondered if Captain Rhonn knew or had guessed about Eleanor. If he had, she knew she was dead meat. He could stick in the fork and see if she were done. Tru shuddered. Her whole life was going down some crazy rabbit hole, and all she could do was stand by helplessly and watch it sink out of sight.

"Damn it, Tru. I said get in here!" Rhonn bellowed from his desk. His voice reverberated through the open door and across the wide space that held the detective unit's cubicles.

The city had saved money by not painting the office area since before Tru received her promotion three years ago. The walls were a dirty yellow accented by gray cubicle separations. City interior designers had placed the cubicles in the uncluttered expanse under the pretension of helping the detectives to achieve new heights of productivity. The effect of the five-foot gray dividers had actually been to separate, berate, and intimidate the detectives. Even the city jail cells were roomier in comparison.

Finding one's way through the maze housing two secretaries, support staff, file cabinets, copy cubicle, and fourteen detectives almost defied even the most determined visitor's ability. The fluorescent lights that glared out of the ceiling next to airflow vents were more likely to circulate the latest influenza contagion than the intended fresh air. The blue industrial carpets set off the area by making it look like a fast-food restaurant gone awry. The room was its own little lower-level prison rather than an investigative division.

In the old days, not that long ago, the office had been a bustle of activity. People moving about, getting things done, talking to one another, helping one another, or simply enjoying the companionship of work. Movement had been the rule of the day. Movement meant life, activity, and productivity. It was noisy and terribly human. The former captain had often closed his window blinds to keep his own visual distractions down to a minimum. The open line of sight for the detectives had provided connection to the jobs being done and the knowledge that they were not alone in their struggles. They knew what the others were going through.

The new system was different. Very different. It had been manufactured for sweatshop minions and worker bees. The administrators had promised that the design would be quiet, aid concentration, and promote a sense of individual self-worth. A lot of other multisyllabic bureaucratic jargon announced the foregone decision. Actually the whole layout was ingenious. Nonmovement and monitored movement was the rule of the day. Detectives were expected to remain at their desks looking productive while making phone calls, entering or receiving information from the computer terminal, preparing reports, and performing other minutiae of the new quota system. If someone rose to leave, the slight cubicle walls would show the top of a head and signal any potentially nonproductive movement to the captain. And the captain would sit, like a straw boss at the edge of the field, overlooking the expanse of his domain. He could call and bring into question what a detective was up to and why. All it took was a flash of hair, a wave of coat, or the stretch of an arm in the aisle to raise his curiosity. And woe be it if he did not like or understand what he saw. He would immediately order the transgressor into his inner sanctum. The office complex had become compartmentalization, work saturation terrorization, and isolation for the rank and file.

Tru rose from her desk. She could sense the attention of the other detectives on her as she crossed the room. She couldn't see them, but she knew they were listening. For a few seconds everything was quiet, then just as quickly she heard the clicking of computer keys and shuffling of paper that dismissed her from their thoughts. They could not afford to feel pity. They would only feel relief that she and not one of them was on the receiving end of what they called the "wrath of Rhonn."

Tru passed the desks of the two detectives nearest the captain's door. They studiously avoided her eyes as she walked near their exposed work areas. They shifted papers and studiously avoided any chance of contact with Rhonn's next victim. Tru caught herself before she giggled. She couldn't be angry with them. They had to live with the new captain too. No one wanted to engage the condemned for fear the condition might be contagious. It had become a way of life. You were on your own and alone. It was sick. It warped the once loyal, bright, and close companions, but there was nothing to do about it. The appointing authorities would not counter their appointee's rules or undermine his command. He had managed to convince them that he was in the process of taking a crew of disorderly, malingering detectives and shaping them into a trim, slim, tight sleuthing machine. Tru had no idea what that meant to the bureaucracy but she did know that those in power had warmed to the idea and allowed the captain to have his way. A ship's crew might mutiny, but petty bureaucrats rarely did.

"Close the door," Rhonn ordered Tru.

He leaned back in his chair and clasped his hands behind the close-cut, expertly cropped hair. His expensive dark-blue jacket and slacks were complemented by a light sea-green shirt; his tie was held tightly in place by a miniature gold badge. He washed his gaze over her appraisingly as she waited. He noted her neat trim figure. He liked sleekness in his women; he only wished she wore dresses. He preferred women in dresses. Dresses made them more appealing and less authoritarian looking. Authoritarian women were hierarchical misfits in his reckoning of the universe, and for that reason he found Tru's general demeanor objectionable.

Captain Rhonn admired Tru's physique. He considered her petiteness and symmetry saving graces.

Her size made her look vulnerable, like any other tasty morsel of femininity. He narrowed his eyes and looked at Tru as a man who was about to enjoy his lunch.

"Sir?" Tru said uncertainly, wanting to get over whatever was going to happen. She thought that a quick professional death would be preferable and less painful to a prolonged probationary torment. She squared her shoulders, deciding that whatever he had in mind, she'd prefer to take it between the eyes and standing.

"Have you read the Southwick report?" He stared at her steadily. His left hand came down from the back of his perfectly shaped square head and smoothed his tie flat to the rock-hard chest beneath the shirt. He had well-manicured nails. The only jewelry he sported was a simple gold wedding band on his left hand. His hands represented the rest of him, large and smooth skinned. He was a fastidious and natty dresser, a trademark that had served him well in his career. At six feet, he wasn't particularly tall for a man, but he had groomed himself in the movement and poise that had secured him advantage over the less careful and less calculating of his colleagues. Slow and unimaginative, he had managed to attract the attention and blessings of his superiors by being dogged, predictable, and obedient. He had floated above controversy by being clever enough never to let blame or fault attach itself to him. Where others dared, he waited; where others intrigued, he stole their thunder; and while others gave credit, he kept it for himself. His contemporaries, those less pliant to organizational preferences, more daring and personally assertive, had been the ones to throw themselves on the barbed barricades to integrity. Rhonn was untroubled by such motivations. He had no personal integrity other than that which would see that he remained promotion material. He had made an art of manipulating weakness and valiant principles then ducking when repercussions hit the fan. Rhonn floated ever onward and upward in the department. A lot less like cream and a lot more like shit. The color of his eyes.

"Yes, I was just getting through the preliminary scene report. Dickenson, of records, gave it to me this morning," Tru said as she remained standing. She knew better than to lower herself into any chair until he gave permission. She'd seen other detectives make that mistake during the first few months of Rhonn's regime. She wasn't about to give him the opportunity to tell her to get her butt off the chair and to endure a lecture about decorum or professional etiquette. Tru believed that the very promotable Rhonn must have missed the department's supervisory training about employee empowerment.

"Good. I'm assigning the case to you."

"But I don't understand . . ." Tru began.

"Of course you don't understand. That's why I want to talk to you." Rhonn smiled wickedly. "That's why you're still a detective grade-two instead of a grade-three or -four after three years in this division. But perhaps most of that can be explained by your receding youth and negligible experience," he said, waiting for the cut to sink in. He wanted to see what she would do. If she shrank or struck out, he'd know that much more about her and how to manipulate her.

Tru looked at him and narrowed her eyes in

loathing. She imagined a hair-trigger sight slightly above the bridge of his nose. Half a grin spread across her lips, and she smirked at him.

Rhonn was surprised at the smile resting easily on Tru's face. It was not what he'd expected. He didn't like the way the grin made her look. The slight baring of teeth gave her face the impression of rapaciousness.

Clearing his throat, he continued. "Some of it might be explained from the fact that you finished in the bottom half of the academy class. You were borderline then, and your performance these last three months seems to be a repetition of that less-than-sterling performance," Rhonn said, trying to warm back up to his task.

Tru was startled by his rudeness and the thin line of harassment he crossed again, all of which he safely performed without a witness available.

"I've had some difficulties, I admit, but . . ." Tru began, not wanting to go over the all-too-plowed ground again.

Rhonn didn't give her a chance. He cut her off in midsentence. "You bet you've had some difficulties. The Dover case is the first and best example that leaps to mind. Additionally, other than that little fiasco in which you were saved further humiliation by two passing patrol units, there's been the condition of your follow-up reports on more cases than I care to recount."

Dover again, Tru sighed inwardly. Her mind flashed back to a scruffy Terry Dover standing over her as she lay crumpled on the ground.

* * * * *

Dover had made a bold daylight robbery of an upscale clothing store in the plaza area. Tru had been lucky or unlucky enough to be having lunch with Eleanor that day. They'd been seated a few doors down at an open-air restaurant when she heard shots ring out. Tru had watched as Dover broke through the doors to dash headlong down the sidewalk.

Tru had rushed from the parasoled table, leaving Eleanor screaming at her to stop and come back. Tru shouted for her to call for backup as she raced after the fleeing figure. She'd spotted Dover running through traffic and brandishing his weapon at hapless motorists as he bounded across the street into a puny alley. Drawing her gun, she darted through the startled-to-slowness traffic and rushed down the alley after him.

It had been a foolish headlong plunge. She had halted barely five feet into the murky shadows of the buildings. She crouched and pressed herself close to a wall. Holding her breath to hear any movement ahead of her, she'd eased herself along the wall. She crouched and remained still, letting her eyes adjust to the wash of shadows. Sirens sounded in the distance and assured her that help was on its way. No other sound disturbed the air. The long thin alley stretched ominously beneath the tall darkening peaks of the buildings. She thought briefly about the prim, moneyed patrons of the plaza who may have paid an unwarrantedly high and brutal price for having more money than sense. She didn't want to lose Dover, so she rose and began to run in a quick dogtrot among the scattered papers, trash receptacles, and empty boxes scattered against the close walls.

She never saw it coming. The short narrow door was recessed in the west side of the building. Afterward, Tru could vaguely remember looking down at her feet to sidestep the goosenecked water pipe that had protruded from the wall. She thought she remembered making a short leap to land on the other side. But before she landed, the world had exploded in her head from the hammering blow from the butt of Dover's gun.

Still clutching her .45 in her right hand, she fell hard onto the wet cobbled pavement. She was vaguely aware of her predicament as she opened her smarting eyes and saw Dover's image wavering above her.

He stood over her, grinning as he brought his gun up and aimed it at the center of her forehead. She could see the bullets slowly rotate in the revolver as he pulled back on the trigger.

"Bye, baby," Dover had said coolly to her.

The world slowed to a trickle of time as Tru watched the hammer cocking back on the .38. In that last instant all she could think was how appropriate he looked dressed out in his black cowboy drover's coat, jeans, boots, and dirty denim shirt. At twenty-three he hadn't changed much from the thirteen-year-old tough she'd arrested ten years ago when she'd been a juvenile officer. He looked as though his career hadn't been any easier on him than hers had been on her. She decided she didn't like the assignment as an epitaph, but by the looks of things she wasn't going to have a choice.

Tru knew she could be killed. Knew she could die in the tiny half-darkened alley with only one clear and ringing thought repeating itself to her over and over, Stupid. Stupid, stupid. It would be more than a little embarrassing to explain it to the goddess when she met her.

Time slowed to a crawl. In reflex Tru jerked her arm up and fired. Her bullet grazed his head, whipping off a two-inch slice of skin as it otherwise flew harmlessly past him. The searing surprise staggered him, and suddenly his chest exploded as Tru looked on in amazement. Belatedly, the trick of sound caught up to the passing bullets and rang in Tru's ears. They'd torn through the dirty denim shirt and echoed viciously in the minuscule canyon of brick.

Pain and surprise flooded across Dover's face and he teetered forward and turned to Tru in silent appeal as he collapsed like a broken doll on top of her. The responding patrol officers who had killed Dover pulled him off. They called for an ambulance as she dazedly leaned against the brick wall. Blood from her head wound flowed slowly down her face.

Eleanor had been sympathetic, even solicitous, but it hadn't changed her demands or demeanor. The incident further served to exacerbate the problems in their relationship by providing Eleanor with a cause by which to rankle Tru. Eleanor had insisted that Tru get into another line of work. Eleanor had particularly insisted on any type of work that would be safer, with traditional hours and fewer demands on time, body, and mind. Something by which Eleanor could more intimately control Tru. Another kind of death. Slower, no less painful, and just as certain as Dover's bad intent.

* * * * *

"North, North! You still with me?" Rhonn demanded. He pounded his hand on the desk. "I'm talking to you."

"Sorry, sir," Tru muttered. "I only meant, I don't really know anything about bombs. Point is, I don't know why you'd want me assigned to the case."

"I'm coming to that." Rhonn shifted in his chair and leaned forward to clasp his hands in front of him patronizingly. "We have reason to suspect this incident might be related to a bombing that happened a year ago in Olathe, Kansas. Same kind of packaging, same kind of explosive, but with a little less devastating effects. It's by no means a perfect match, but close enough for government work. In that one, however, the poor bastard lived minus most of his face and all his right hand."

Tru shuddered at the image. Sometimes she couldn't remember or imagine what had possessed her to go into law enforcement. Visions of pain and destruction tormented and haunted her every time she pursued a case. Her mother had suggested nursing as a profession, but Tru knew wouldn't have been able to stand those daily doses of pain and blood. Bedpans had put her off too. In law enforcement she'd managed to use her revulsion to drive her imagination and help her find perpetrators. She didn't particularly like it, but she was good at it. She liked being good at her job, and that was all that mattered to her.

"I'm putting you on the case because of that three-week FBI training course in serial murder you took last year. Might as well start earning your keep and repaying the department for the money we've put into you," Rhonn said as he reached across his walnut desk and absently fingered a stack of memos.

His office was immaculate. Tru had heard he'd purchased his own furniture to satisfy his dark, conservative tastes and to place himself at the center of the image he worked at perfecting. Brooding colors of burgundy, forest green, and tiny trimmings of black had been blended on the walls. Mahogany-framed hunting scenes tastefully poised at just the right height in just the right places made the setting impeccable. There were no personal artifacts except the usual copies of diplomas, modest training certificates, and letters of appreciation from local politicos. Nothing in the room spoke about the individual noncompany side of the man. He was not a braggart; it was not his intention to impress or inform his subordinates. He considered subordinates useless except for what rewards their accomplishments might bring him. Rhonn was a closed book except to those who he believed might be able to do him good — his superiors and the political friends he'd been grooming over the last twenty years.

"The FBI course I took was good, of course, Captain," Tru half stammered, "but the point of the matter is, it was just one course. You have other detectives who have been more intensely and thoroughly trained, not to mention who are more experienced in this sort of thing. I want to do a good job, but Jones, with his military experience in explosives, is better equipped to do the right thing here," Tru said, hating the sound of her own voice. It seemed unsure, small, and uncertain. She didn't know where it had come from, but she knew it wasn't her own. It sounded like another gift Eleanor had bequeathed her.

What she wanted to do was ask the captain for a needed vacation. Over the last four months she had squirreled away three weeks of overtime. New sights and sounds might revive her and her spirits.

"He's already assigned to it and partnered with Jenkins. I want you on this too. You won't be working this with them, however. You're going to be my independent, the fresh perspective, so to speak. It will also give me a means of more accurately evaluating you. I don't know if you realize it or not, but you're on thin ice. I hate to be hasty about personnel decisions, and I want to do right by you. You have a lot of possibilities and potential. This is your chance to prove yourself." He smiled at her and waved for her to sit in the chair.

"What do you mean, 'prove myself'?" Tru asked slowly. She didn't like the way the conversation was going.

"Just that," he said, ignoring her rejection of the offered chair. Rhonn stretched himself confidently and pulled a file out of the middle drawer on his desk. "Your performance ratings have been so poor for the last six months that the top brass wants me to do a special evaluation on you. I wouldn't be able to properly do it if I had you partnered up with someone, now would I?" He paused for effect.

"Sir?" Tru couldn't believe her ears and rejected what her mind wanted to tell her. She knew about Rhonn's special evaluations. Three detectives during the last year had been the subject of his special evaluations. None of their careers had survived the review. Not even her friend Timothy.

Timothy Youghons had been the last person subjected to a Rhonn "special." It had begun two months before he resigned. Youghons had been more closeted than Tru. Some of his fellow detectives might have suspected he was gay, but no one other than Tru had known for certain. He and Tru had befriended each other three years ago as quickly and as surely as birds of a feather might identify each other. They'd just received their promotions. During his last two months with the department, Timothy had often joked that he had always tried to be a pillar of discretion in the gay and lesbian community of Kansas City. A necessary fact of life in the midwest small town propensities of Kansas City, Missouri.

He had experienced some very bad luck and a messy falling out with his current attraction shortly before Rhonn's special evaluation. One day, Timothy was simply no longer there. Everything he owned had disappeared from his desk. After his resignation, the rumors had flown about whom and what Timothy had preferred sexually. Rhonn had seen to it that Timothy had not been allowed to leave with his reputation as an investigator intact. It had become a simple and debilitating fact of life that when Rhonn made you a project, everything hidden had the nasty habit of becoming revealed. Tru had learned that Timothy had been given the choice to resign or face the ostracism of the detective unit. It was a career buster, and Rhonn had enjoyed his work.

Tru knew the top brass never paid enough

attention to general staff issues to ever want a special evaluation on anyone in the department. The brass had to be coaxed into wanting a special by the persistence of a supervising officer. It was a setup, and Tru knew she was Rhonn's next target. She didn't want to imagine that the special might have something to do with her being a lesbian. Was Rhonn a witch-hunter or merely an overzealous manager? Tru struggled with the question. No, she thought, he'd fired or requested resignations from others who were not homosexual. Regardless, she knew she didn't need or want more complications in her life. Not now. For that matter, not ever. A sinking feeling spread up from the pit of her stomach and grabbed her by the throat.

"If I were you I'd dust off those training modules, read the reports, and develop a plan of action for your investigative endeavors, Detective North. Give the other cases you're working on to Charlie and Fred over in sex and checks. You're on this one full-time starting ten minutes ago. Is that clear?" Rhonn snapped shut the folder with Tru's name written across it.

"Perfectly," Tru said.

"You're dismissed," Rhonn said curtly as Tru started to walk out the door. "And keep in touch."

"Approximately?" Tru said, knowing the routine.

"Approximately, every two weeks. More, if you really have anything to say that might be worth hearing," Rhonn said. As he reached for the phone, a wry smile crossed his lips. He was a patient man. He figured he had all the time he needed to set her up and watch her fall. He'd picked the most outlandish assignment he could think of for her. He was confident in the outcome. She'd struggle, flounder, and collapse under the weight and complexity of the case. There wasn't a case to make. There were no leads. It was virtually unsolvable and a perfect scenario by which to evaluate her.

He'd been watching her go through a slow disintegration for some time. Regardless of the physical appeal, he'd never liked her. But she wasn't fighting him, challenging him, or calling him on his treatment. Recently it seemed as though something had happened to her. She was more pliable now, and it was an advantage he could use. He didn't care what had happened, where, or with whom. It made her more entertaining than she had been. She'd been too proud, too self-assured, and quietly challenging to his authority. He'd had to work to keep her in line with his personal vision of what a female detective should be. As far as he was concerned, she belonged in the juvenile division or as a matron in a nice cozy women's jail.

He had sensed her growing personal and professional skepticism. It had become transparent under his scrutiny. He'd give her time and rope and have her begging for demotion to parking-meter detail or leaving to find a more suitably traditional woman's job. He wanted the best for her but not in his division. He'd give Miss Tru North time to screw up and then allow her to leave the business of law enforcement to her betters. He liked the new and vulnerable Tru. He would use that vulnerability. He knew he'd win. Unconsciously he licked his lips, tasting his triumph.

Chapter 4

Nine o'clock Saturday night Tru sat back from her desk at home and closed the covers on the bomb investigation file copies she'd been poring over. She'd been making swift little notes and outlines in the notebook she had dedicated to the case. Her eyes burned, and she rubbed them wearily. Looking at the clock on the mantel, she speculated briefly about going out to clear her head. The second the thought crossed her mind, her stomach dropped a notch as she recalled bits and pieces of her last Friday night's escapade at the Round Table Bar.

"More like round heels," Tru commented derisively to the room. She picked up her gray cat, Poupon, and stroked his soft fur for comfort. He purred back happily at her. Friday night was a distant, half-forgotten blur. After she had gotten home, she'd tried to drown her self-loathing in additional doses of bourbon. The fog she'd slipped into had scared her the next morning. Her immediate memory of the bar was agonizingly unclear. She knew that a tendency to drink to oblivion was a dangerous sign and a sign she knew she needed to heed.

The following Saturday morning had hit her like a wrecking ball aimed at the back of her head. Her mouth had tasted as though a weary battalion of amazons had changed socks in it. None of it compared to what her head and stomach did to her during the short time she managed to be awake during that long day. Cowardice and nausea caused her to conduct a search-and-destroy for the leftover painkillers her dentist had prescribed after a root canal last year. She'd been fairly certain the medication and the alcohol swimming along in her bloodstream wouldn't kill her. Not positive, but almost certain and far past caring. She took the pills. When she came around to wakefulness again it was dark. She had managed to heat a can of chicken soup and return to bed to wait for Sunday morning.

It had worked, almost. Sunday morning she awoke feeling annoyingly human. She confirmed her presence in the real world by going to the gym. After a short, intense workout, she let the steaming sauna leach the rest of the impurities from her body. It had been partially perfect. The imperfections were in her memory. No effort of will, chant, or relaxation technique would let her forget the intoxicating touch of the woman she'd let make love to her. Neither will nor volition would let her recall the woman's face, her name, or the happenstance of their meeting. Her memory was a blank. The woman had become a pair of disembodied hands and fingers. Tru was caught between hoping it had been a dream and feverishly hoping it had been real. She wondered if she could or would ever go to the bar again. She'd had a momentary hysterical notion that she might never again be able to go to any of the other women's bars in town. The off chance of not knowing she was meeting the other woman alarmed her. What if she did meet her again and the other woman reminded her? What if she met her and the other woman didn't remind her? What would she say? How could she say anything? What could she possibly say? Surrendering to another lost cause, Tru finally landed a peremptory strike promising herself she'd not go back to the Round Table again in this lifetime. She acknowledged embarrassingly that even if she couldn't recall the full details of the evening, the other patrons might. She didn't want to chance seeing the story repeated in their eyes. Tru would let it be the mystery it had become and hope that the whole regrettable incident would recede as a silent twinging regret.

Stop it and stop it right now, she commanded wearily to herself. The loathing and bitterness would only serve to increase her sense of helplessness. She had to get hold of herself soon or face downward spiraling as a very real prospect.

But I want to go out, she complained plaintively to herself. *I've been good all week. I can be good tonight. Once doesn't make a drunk does it? Or, is that what they all say?* A frown creased her forehead.

"I'll take a shower. That will help, won't it, Poupon?" Tru asked as the cat stretched himself in typical disregard. "That's what I thought."

In the shower Tru let the water run over her body and pound her with sweet exhilarating relief. The French milled soap refreshed her mind, body, and senses. She'd abandoned her thoughts about the bombing cases and let herself drift in the steamy delight of rushing hot water. She lingered, letting her hands soap and clean every surface, swell, and hollow of her body. As she closed her eyes, other hands seemed to join hers. Hands she had known. Hands she wanted to feel again. Hands of a mystery she knew she'd never have the courage to unravel.

"Fool," she whispered and let the hot water chase away the figment of imagination.

Forty minutes later, freshly showered and revived, Tru finished dressing. As she sat on the edge of the bed lacing her boots, she knew the jeans and cambric shirt would not be out of place where she was going. She stood and walked bravely toward the door. "Don't wait up for me unless you really want to," she called back to Poupon as she locked the door.

Thirty minutes later, Tru took a deep breath and stepped inside Tres Florets. The music was softer at Tres Florets than it ever was at the Round Table. Tru breathed a sigh of relief; this was going to be better. Quieter music, distant companions, and a way of killing a little time without getting killed back. Squinting and trying to focus as she walked down the short dark hall to the interior, Tru didn't see

George and almost knocked him off his bouncer's high stool.

"Hey, sweetie, slow down. There's plenty of time and plenty of ladies inside. No need to go butch on me," George chided.

"Sorry, George. I forgot. The hallway just seems to end so abruptly," Tru said as she recognized his familiar voice. The dark shadows of the bar hid his face.

"Tru! Is that you, truly you, Tru dear?" George mocked her in habitual banter. "Let me turn this light on," he said, reaching for the light string on the old podium near the doorway. The indirect lights at the back only brought the bar and bartender into sharp relief. Muted lights hung from the ceiling; their blues and golds cast the patrons into subtly shaded silhouettes. It was a cast of specters but Tru didn't mind. Everything and everyone was slightly invisible, and she'd had her share of exposure at the Round Table.

"Hush!" Tru said sharply. "No need to announce me to the place." Tru felt a blush go to her face as George turned back from the obscured patrons hunkering at the bar.

Smiling ferociously, George swept her up in a one-armed embrace and called out to the bartender. "Hey, Doris! Set one up for me and my own Tru love, sweet little Tru." George grinned mischievously down at her from his gangly six feet four.

Tru could see several heads of the half-dozen or so men and women at the bar turn and briefly look in their direction. She decided to ignore them. She couldn't see them well enough to recognize anyone.

The light was poor, and she'd been out of circulation a long time. She knew the long-term customers had grown used to George's occasional outbursts of guest appreciation. It was part of the free entertainment and his trademark. He didn't do it often, but when he did he did it lavishly and all in fun. Part of a regular's fun was waiting to see who his next victim might be. Tonight he had Tru.

Doris the bartender was a huge aging amazon who looked like she could still take on the whole First Armored Division. She waved fondly at George and Tru. George and Doris had bought the bar twenty years ago as a hedge against time and old age. They had managed to make it a going concern. Doris ran the money end, and it was George's job to run the customers. It had worked well for them in temperaments and financial success. They had made their bar a haven against rancor, noise, and melancholy. It was appreciated in the community and supported for its benefits.

Doris turned to the liquor lining the wall, nodding her head in compliance with George's request.

"Stop it, George. I just came in for a quiet drink," Tru said, resisting his insistence just enough to not disappoint him. She hoped she'd passed muster.

"This is a disco, dearie, not the mountains. If you want quiet, you'll have to go to the dark side of the mood. Or is that *moon*?" George saw the look on Tru's face and quickly lowered his voice. "Well, if that's what you want to do, you can. But you can't do it just right this minute because your reappearance is a special occasion. What did that bad old Eleanor do to you anyway? Hole you up in a box —

no pun intended — and not let you out unless you cried mercy?" George joked and chatted nonstop as he steered Tru to the bar and signaled a free waiter to take over for him at the door.

"Not exactly," Tru cringed. "And not anymore," she said in confession as her throat constricted. She turned away from George and the look that had crossed Doris's face when she set the beer in front of her on the counter.

"Oh, honey," George said and pulled her to his chest holding her sincerely. "I'm sorry. You all right? What happened?" He fired the questions at her in quick succession. Pulling up a stool for Tru to sit on, he motioned to Doris.

"Not now, not here. Maybe not in this lifetime." Tru resisted his pull for her to sit.

George looked around the bar and, reaching down to pat Tru's hand, said, "Come on. I'll buy you the next drink too. Let's go over and sit in a booth where we can have some privacy. Then you can tell Uncle George all about it." His voice softly pulled Tru away from the stool he'd offered.

His hand resting on her shoulder, George pointed Tru toward an empty booth at the back of the bar. As they walked the length of the long bar, Tru noticed a woman sitting with her back turned to her and George. The woman seemed to be intently watching Tru and her escort in the mirrors behind the bar. Tru felt their eyes meet briefly in the glass and somber shadows and walked past her. But George's body and the dimness of the bar conspired to hide the woman's face and prevent Tru from getting a clear look at the woman. The woman's figure was backlit, and Tru had difficulty noticing anything other than the wide shoulders. In the haloing light of the bar, Tru knew she probably wouldn't even have been able to recognize Eleanor. Tru shrugged inwardly. Of course the woman was watching. She was watching the dance floor in the other room through the wide arched doorway she and George had passed through on their way to the booths. Tru chuckled bitterly at her overinflated opinion of her attractiveness to other women. She wondered briefly whether believing people were staring at her would be the only warning signal she'd get of impending insanity. Maybe it wouldn't be too bad, she speculated. A little certain, slow insanity. She wouldn't miss her life with Eleanor, her life in the police department, or her life as someone capable of loving and being loved in return. Tru shook the thought away and slid into the booth George had steered her toward.

"My back's to the door, George. You know I don't like to sit like this," Tru said, feeling the hackles go up on the back of her neck.

"Police paranoia, my dear. Old-fashioned, highly commercialized, and boring police paranoia. You've been watching too many movies," George assured her. "Now just sit quiet, gather yourself, take a long draw from that drink, and tell me what's been happening in your world that has left you so bruised."

George was patient. He let Tru sit across from him and slowly sip the beer Doris had brought her. Occasionally, while her quietude persisted, he'd reach over and pat the hands that she clutched around her drink. He silently watched the patrons enter and leave in clusters, pairs, and singles while waiting for Tru to speak. At one point, he nodded briefly to a woman who had eased herself off a bar stool and walked over to sit in the booth directly behind Tru. Fleetingly, he wondered if she was waiting for her lover to come through the door, and he hoped the woman would not be disappointed. George was a romantic. He hated to see anyone alone. He glanced back at Tru. It made his heart ache to see her in such a congested state of pain.

"It's nothing, George, or at least there's nothing I can do about it," Tru said vehemently as she tossed herself back into the cushioned back of the booth.

George winced and wondered if the woman on the other side of the double-backed cushion bench had been jarred. He didn't want to get into a cat fight on bar manners with a woman who had looked as capable as she did. Her movements were sure and certain, with a particularly predatory ambling style. He hated to get into pissing contests with the serious butch types. He knew they might win the round with him, but they'd lose the war to Doris. George relaxed when neither sound nor protest came from the other side.

"Nothing is ever nothing. So, we'll just see about that," George persisted with Tru. "Now tell me what's been going on with you."

"Simply put?" Tru bit the words off and spit them out as quickly as she could. "Eleanor can't tolerate me and left . . . no, I left. My life is a mess. My job just got put on the line. My boss is after my hide. And I've been put on notice by life on all counts."

"Whoa, that's quite a recitation. First things first. Tell me about you and Eleanor," George encouraged.

"What's to tell? When I said she couldn't tolerate

me, I meant it. I moved out four weeks ago, but not before she made it very plain why I had to leave."

Tru felt a hammer slam into her heart as she recalled the words Eleanor had used. "I," Tru gasped, the razor-edged words slashing her anew. "I, she said I wasn't sexually interesting enough or pretty enough and was too male identified because I'm a cop and work with men doing the dirty work of the patriarchy. Because of my fascist leanings, I'm too rigid to ever appeal to a real woman except as an object of pity. She said she'd only been being kind to me and . . . and had been pretending that what she felt was love for me. She said she had thought she could bring me around." The words came as a torrent. She didn't know if she could stop them, didn't know what she'd do if she stopped talking. She didn't dare feel anything but the pain. It was real, and she needed something real to help her stay alive. It was all she had left. Anything else would be too dangerous.

Tru stopped. Tears welled up in her eyes, and her throat was trying to choke her to death. George held her hands. He was shaken at what he heard. He wondered how even the Eleanor he knew could have been so vicious. He'd known Tru since she was eighteen, when she first tried to sneak into his bar. She'd been a likable kid. He'd not met many kinder or more sensitive in the years since.

"Oh, baby," George crooned. "Poor baby." George could feel his temper rising in hot vindictiveness toward Eleanor. She deserved something special the next time he saw her. He wasn't certain what it might be, but he was sure she had earned it.

"Oh . . . that's not . . ." Tru swallowed to keep from drowning with each word. "That's not all. She said, because of my deficiencies, that's what she called them, because of my deficiencies, she'd had to depend on other women to help remind her what making woman-to-woman love was about. She told me it had been necessary because I was a lie and had no feelings for a woman who sincerely loved women. She said I was a sick, demented pretender and she should have never trusted me with her emotions."

"My lord." George forced himself to remain calm so he could hear everything Tru needed to say. He felt a rising urgency to find shelter for Tru. He knew that no one should have to stand that kind of pain or be made to feel that alone and unvalued. He had seen other friends emotionally disintegrate under less malicious attacks than the one Eleanor had heaped on Tru. George had known Eleanor had a streak of maliciousness in her, but now he knew she was crazy mean as well.

"Oh, George, she might be right," Tru said, and she signaled Doris for another drink. "We hadn't touched in months. Every time I reached for her, she shrank away with some chilling excuse. I haven't been touched or felt loved in months . . . then, that's not quite true, but . . . Eleanor wanted to let me know why she hated me before she left. She wanted to hurt . . . and she did, George. She did a pretty good job." Tru slumped exhausted into the cushioned booth.

"I lied. I have been touched, but that . . . that was a drunken freakish accident. Fits doesn't · it?" Tru looked up to see George's eyebrow rise in anticipation. "There's no need to go into it. I can't remember who she was. Don't ask me. But I think it proves the point that Eleanor was making and that she was probably more right than she knew," Tru said defeatedly.

"Come on. You had a fling, a little dalliance to help you make sure you were still alive. Or, maybe you wondered if Eleanor left you anything to feel with. Don't agree with Eleanor. That would be what she wants. She can't stand it unless she leaves smoke and ash in her path," George affirmed.

"I know, George, I just feel so, so . . ." Tru faded.

"I know dear. What can I do to help?" George found himself caught between wanting to rock Tru and wanting to find Eleanor and mangle her spiteful neck.

"Nothing, George," Tru said quietly. She sat still for long minutes letting the tears stream down her face. George let her cry and ordered another beer when the last one was dry.

They sat in silence. Being there with her was all George could think of doing. Tru smiled faintly between lapses in the music and tears.

Rousing herself out of the daze, she patted George's hand and covered it with her own. "I've got to go home, George. Sitting here isn't doing me any good. Crying in my beer with or without friendly companionship is not the way to deal with life. I've got to go home," she said in a soft voice. "I'll be fine," Tru said, and stood to go.

"Look, Tru, you can stay at my house. No one's using the spare room. You don't have to be alone," George worried. Friends don't let friends drive heartbroken.

"Yeah, yeah. I do have to be alone. You know my grandfather used to say 'You come in alone and go out alone, so you might as well get use to being alone.' Cynical old fart, wasn't he?" Tru said. She waved good-bye.

George watched anxiously as Tru walked away, nodded briefly at Doris, and disappeared down the hallway. He regretted his inaction. "I don't like the feel of this. That's no way to treat a lady," George said to the space where Tru had been sitting.

"It certainly is not," came a response from the other side of the booth. The tall woman stretched out of the booth, turned, and let her eyes meet his. Fierce concentration and assertiveness on her face bore into him.

George was struck by her solid good looks. Tall, but not overly so, with a grace that would have done a panther proud. She moved, looking first at the exit and then back at George. Her auburn hair rode full and easily on her head. Irish to the quick. She nodded at him and walked out of the bar.

Marki cautiously followed Tru to her house. It wasn't hard. Tru was trying to be an alert driver, conscious of her drinking. She'd been slow to get to her car and was driving herself slowly home. Marki didn't want her to know she was behind her. She simply didn't want her to come to further harm. She wasn't sure what to do except to wait and watch Tru get home alive without causing harm to herself.

Marki parked and waited outside Tru's apartment. She watched the lights go on and saw Tru's shadow pass restlessly across the curtains. Finally the lights went out, and at four in the morning Marki was satisfied that Tru had gone safely to bed. She wanted her safe. She wanted the chance to know her and was determined she would make it happen.

Chapter 5

Tru turned her unmarked car onto I-35 South and pushed the accelerator to the floor. It was the only way to safely merge with the traffic pattern as it hurled toward Olathe. Olathe, Kansas, had once been a sleepy little farm town ignored by the moneyed majority east of the river. That was twenty years ago. Now Olathe, quaintly known as "land of the little trees" because of the new housing developments, sat in the heart of the rising Johnson County enterprise. Major manufacturers, entrepreneurs, corporate headquarters, and chain stores scattered in unbroken plots blurred the distinction between urban, suburban, and rural.

It was boom business, the nouveau riche, and all their flashes of quick money. The business community had decided that Olathe was just their cup of tea and invaded the town, changing it forever. It became the next move toward suburbanization. Chrome and glass, black steel, brick, and marble courtyards replaced sheds and barns.

It was a suburban sprawl linked by the arms of the interstate system that raged with trucks, cars, and RVs. Everyone was going somewhere and doing it at a terrific speed.

Tru fought for her space on the six-lane and navigated with a skill brought on by survival instinct. It was the only way to drive on the interstate. It was a way of life.

The newly remodeled city hall housed the main offices of the Olathe police department. The exterior of the building had been thoroughly reworked to match the surrounding burgundy stone of the judicial offices. The administrative offices and special investigation units of the police department were housed on the fifth floor down a series of unpredictable turns and corners. Having to stop and ask for directions twice made Tru wonder if the building's architect had a penchant for mazes. She decided that whatever the fee had been for the design, it had been too much.

Finally finding the right office doors, Tru stepped into a small anterior waiting room. She found herself staring at a receptionist who was safely ensconced behind bombproof and bulletproof glass with concrete-and-steel fortification.

"May I help you?" the receptionist mouthed. Her

voice floated over Tru's head and hung in the air. Tru looked away from the receptionist to the speaker system in the ceiling. When she looked back, the receptionist smiled and nodded. Tru couldn't make up her mind whether to address the ceiling or the face behind the glass. She chose the glass.

"I'm Detective North with the Kansas City, Missouri, police department." She held up her badge and ID for the receptionist. "I have an appointment with your Detective Fred Quire."

"Certainly, Detective North. I'll ring him to come get you." The receptionist nodded to Tru and toward one of the knockoff Queen Anne chairs decorating the tiny lobby as she silently punched Detective Quire's call number into the office intercom system.

Tru waited as patiently as she could and took in her surroundings. It was amazing to find Queen Anne chairs, gentle gray carpeting, and walnut-framed pastoral settings inside the tight little bunker. It was mind-boggling to try to match the high security with the haughtiness of the room. Tru sighed and decided that the interior decorator had been a friend of the mad architect.

A door opened and a small, dumpy middle-aged man walked in. He nodded once at the receptionist, who then gestured toward Tru.

"Hello," he said cordially. "I'm Detective Fred Quire, and you must be Ms. North."

"Detective North," Tru said, rising and extending her hand.

"Of course. Well, I was expecting someone older."

"I am, by the minute," Tru smiled.

"Well, anyway, come with me, and we'll see if we can do each other any good on this thing."

He held the door open for Tru to return down the maze she'd just traveled as he thudded silently beside her.

"First, I thought your offices were in there," Tru said, pointing back toward the reception area.

"Hardly. That's administration. They don't want the bomb boys in there. They consider us far too dangerous and noisy. Besides, you have to be a big desk-rider to work in there. Something I hope never to become."

"But the signs . . . ?"

"Just to confuse the masses. We're located in the basement. Silly, isn't it," Quire chuckled.

The elevator descended rapidly. As it came to a rest, the doors opened to a room of cubicles, gray carpeting, fluorescent lights, and a small scattering of brick-walled rooms stationed at the far end of the expanse.

"Looks like home," Tru grunted.

"Yeah? Well, if it does, it makes you wonder if government gets some kind of kick or kickback from the ghoul who created these rabbit warrens."

"Interesting thought. 'Course they probably don't care because they don't have to work in them. Which hole is yours?"

"This one. The case material is here for you. I had a secretary make copies of it yesterday." Quire grabbed the file folder on his desk. Tru noticed that there was barely enough room in the cubicle for Quire. She looked around questioningly.

"Take it over there if you want. Joe's out in the field today. He won't mind if you borrow his space. Just don't move anything on his desk; he's funny that way." Quire nodded to the cubicle across the aisle.

"Here's what we've got so far. It's rather slim except for the autopsy report and some graphic photos, if you like that sort of thing," Tru said as she handed Quire a folder from her briefcase.

"Thanks, just what I wanted with my morning coffee."

"Yeah," Tru said settling into Joe's chair. "Talk to you in a few."

Tru thumbed the reports and scratched notes in the margins when an issue or question was raised in her mind. She was grateful to have her own copy. She wouldn't have to rely on memory or disconnected notes when she got back to her office.

The victim's name was John Tanner. He'd been a prizewinning photojournalist and owner of a photo and framing store in one of the local upscale shopping malls. He'd been doing very well for himself before the explosion. Incredibly, he had lived, although Tru wasn't sure living was what he'd ever be able to do again. Without heroic plastic surgery, he might never be able to feel comfortable in public. He would certainly never return to photography.

She rose from the desk twenty minutes later. She'd read all she needed to for the time being. She wanted to ask Quire a few questions and see if he had any thoughts to share with her. He wasn't at his desk. Tru looked around and decided against wandering through the maze of cubicles. The basement was a wide 200-foot by 150-foot open expanse of mundane decoration. She sat in Quire's chair and waited.

While waiting, she closed her eyes and tried to

practice the deep breathing exercises she'd learned from some self-hypnosis tapes she'd been listening to for months. She was frustrated with her progress and with the dead police psychologist who'd bullied her into buying them. She couldn't seem to get it right. She couldn't let go enough to let her mind rest. She squinted her eyes against the glare of lights and tried to recall the rhythm and music of the tapes.

She placed her feet flat on the floor and let her arms rest on her lap. She thought about the gentle breeze of a seashore, the trees softly swaying behind her, and the warmth of the sun as it rose above the cool waters. Tru imagined the rays penetrating her, a light traveling from her toes, legs, and thighs up to her solar plexus. It spread and expanded in her chest, across her arms, up to her face, and finally full on her forehead. She bathed in renewal, peace, and security. She tried to float on a wave of tranquility. She wanted to center herself, to feel the connections, and to let the connectedness soothe the hurts in her life. She needed to heal. Needed to give herself time to feel and be whole again. She gave herself permission to let the healing begin.

"Sleeping on duty, Detective?" a voice over her head boomed into her consciousness.

Tru jerked. Flinging herself out of the chair, her heart raced and face flushed as she turned in embarrassment to meet the eyes of Detective Quire.

"Any chance I get."

"Me too." Quire winked. "What say you and I get a cup of coffee across the street and powwow a little on these blown-up boys?"

"Suits me."

Tru retrieved her briefcase from Joe's office and followed Quire back toward the elevator doors.

The café was a nineteen-fifties remake, a little out of place amongst the smoked-glass fronts of the courthouse area complex. But it was comfortable, and the prices were reasonable. A tired looking waitress greeted them. Quire and Tru were the only people in the café. It suited Tru for privacy and relief from the basement.

The waitress brought coffee and banter to the table. Tru realized that the café was probably a familiar haunt to Quire.

"You show me yours and I'll show you mine," Tru said, as she sat stirring her coffee.

"Pardon me?"

"Tell me some things about Tanner I don't know from reading the report, and I'll tell you about Southwick. Okay?"

"Oh, yeah. Well, to begin with, the man doesn't seem to have an enemy in the world —"

"Except one seriously pissed-off guy."

"Yes, but we don't know that the person who did the deed was a man."

"Really, and how many women do you know who have an ability with any type of explosive ordinance?" Tru countered.

"All right, but there are plenty of ex-cops, lady ex-cops, and military who might. 'Course it didn't used to be that way."

Tru looked at Quire over the rim of her coffee cup.

"It's still not much that way. But, besides that, it's not quite what women do or a typical weapon of

65

choice for women. I think we can safely exclude women and narrow the possibilities. Don't you?"

"More than likely. This guy Tanner has himself a nice little business over at the Packard Shopping Mall. He's won some trophies for his shots of nature scenes and of Colorado firefighters a few years back. He's divorced. Two grown sons, no money trouble, and no lady trouble. Basically, the guy's clean. He's doing fine right up until the day the package blows his face off. Nothing significant."

"That's not much. It's nothing as a matter of fact."

"I know, but it's all we have 'cept for the remains of the box and the lab reports."

"Anything there?"

"It was plastique. A little bit of that goes a long way. It was homemade stuff, usually considered pretty unstable for mixing. After that's the box. A nice piece of work before it shattered all over the guy. My guess is that it was expensive. But why would you buy an expensive piece just to blow it up? I don't know. The bomb detonator itself was a simple device and pretty specific in its finality.

"You saw the photos. There was quite a bit of it left. Simple trigger device. Just open, and boom!" Quire added more sugar to his cooling coffee.

"Ours was much the same. At least along the same lines. The box was different. I guess you could say it might have been pricey. Your bomb maimed and ours killed. Might just have been luck of the draw? If we can speak of luck here."

"What about your guy?"

"Not much to say. Southwick was an artist. He mostly worked in oils but apparently did a little in pen-and-ink. He had something of a reputation regionally. Some of his stuff hangs in a few banks, art shops, and corporate offices in town. Middling success but nothing to send mama singing to the bank. No enemies. Lots of friends and a few scattered lovers. No one with an attitude. As far as we know, the only problem he had was this one."

"Leads like that made our lieutenant put this one on the back burner. Nowhere to go with it, and our guy isn't talking. No chance he ever will. The concussion gave him an instant lobotomy. Good thing, too. If I knew my face had been shaved back to my gums, I'd want to be in la-la land too."

"Nice thought. Thanks for sharing, Quire."

"Don't mention it."

Vivid visualizations popped into her mind's eye. Tru looked at the Danish on her plate and moved it away. She couldn't make the images go away.

"Your lieutenant shelved the case. I thought a rich little town like this would be screaming for blood."

"Would be too, if it had been some well-placed family's kid or local prima Donna or Donnie. Not this one. Just a local who was doing well. People settled into the idea that it was one of those random senseless things. Makes them feel comfortable and safe. As safe as you get with random or senseless."

"How do you feel about that?"

"No choice. We've got lots of other things to do. The case is over a year old, cold as ice, no leads and no guesses. We moved on to things bigger, better and easier, or not, to solve. I figure in another year or two we'll close this one by exception."

"What's the exception?"

"No one knows what to do with it except assume it was a one-time blip on the screen. We don't know what else to do."

"Hell of a way to do business."

"Don't sit there and tell me you guys don't do the very same thing."

"Of course we do. But doesn't it make any difference that we've had a bomber too?"

"Sure might. If you can, tell me what the connection would be?" Quire waved the waitress over to refill their cups.

"Not a clue. Both boxes that exploded were nice looking and well made." Tru struggled to think of instances of match.

"That's a little thin."

"Is, isn't it? Pretty boxes and artist types. Think anything might be there?"

"It sounds like a hole to me. When's the last time you heard about artists waging war with anything other than elaborate insults?"

"I don't know any artists."

"That's not the point. Think about them for a minute. They're namby-pamby, wishy-washy swishes. Boys or girls either one. Not like you and me. We eat nails and dead bodies for breakfast. They're sensitive types. Most of them are starving for attention and starving, period, 'cause they can't get real jobs."

"That's a little hard."

"Maybe," Quire said, shifting his soft bulk in the booth. "Maybe it is hard, but if it's not the truth it's damn close to it. Nothing wrong with it, theirs is a different life and one you don't go finding mad bombers in."

"Some bomber was in the lives of both of these guys."

"Right. But he, or they, had to come from outside these guys' lives. It was a fluke. Maybe a copycat is what you got on your side of the line. Over here the only thing we have is a quasidecapitated photographer. Did your package have a return address on it or a recognizable postmark?"

"No, at least nothing we could find in the mess that was left."

"Us either. These things are separated by distance and time. There's no connection and no hope of connection. All of which makes me wonder what your department is up to." Quire hunched over his coffee like a vulture and stared into Tru's eyes.

"I don't know. Trying to solve this looks grim to me." Tru sighed and drank another sip of her coffee.

"Go home or go back to your office and tell your supervisor to give you something to work on that has a little meat on it. This is a dead end. I ought to know. I've seen plenty of them in my thirty years."

"You, an old fart?" Tru grinned at Quire.

"Yeah, old fart. Fifty-something, and if I'd have saved my money like I was supposed to when I was a pup like you, I'd be pulling the string next year. But no. I tried to make some fast investments and ended up paying for the wrong kind of education." Quire shrugged as he threw his arms along the top of the booth. His little round belly touched the table edge as he arched his back and yawned.

"I'll try to plan better," Tru acknowledged. She smiled at him and wondered if every police detective in the world became a philosopher after a certain age. She shuddered, hoping it wasn't true.

"Good. I've got to get back to the dungeon, and you should get back to yours. Get a real case and have some fun. You don't look like you've been having enough fun. Young thing like you ought to get out more." Quire chucked her on the shoulder as they walked out to the sidewalk.

"Thought that's how you lost your money," Tru protested.

"Did too. But did I mention that I thought it was worth every dime?"

"Is that what I heard?" Tru said, watching Quire walk toward the courthouse.

"I think that's what maybe you should have heard. I love my job. Doesn't mean I wouldn't want to do something different." Quire waved over his shoulder at her and lumbered down the sidewalk.

There was no way she could tell Quire she'd been given a rotten case by an equally rotten supervisor. He might have sympathized, but pity from a stranger was paltry fare. What she needed was a way to look at the case, a new angle, something fresh. It was the only case she had, and her career was riding on it. She was going to have to ride it to the ground.

Chapter 6

Tru drove back to the city, her briefcase bulging with copies of the two bomb reports. She tried to concentrate on her driving as the early afternoon rush north on I-35 proved almost as hazardous as the morning rush. She didn't like trying to split her attention. It was either drive or think about bombs. Something had to give. In irritation she exited near the state line and cruised back toward the city in the more moderate speed zones available. Stoplights were easier to manage. The wait allowed her to ruminate over the precious few details of the case.

She was south of where she wanted to be, but the leisurely pace satisfied her. Tru stayed happily mesmerized by the problems of the bombings for long minutes.

When she came back to awareness, she was surprised to discover she was three blocks from the Landing Café, one of her favorite restaurants. Rhonn had told her to report in once every two weeks or so. Determined to follow his directive, she would not rush back to the office.

She looked at her watch and figured that the noon rush crowd would have left the restaurant. She was in an unmarked car, but no more unmarked than any other detective's car. She knew the locals and anyone else could spot a police department car a mile away. Where to hide the car? Then she remembered the grocery store in the next block and swung neatly into the parking lot at the back.

Inside the restaurant she settled into a comfortable feeling. She'd be able to eat and get a little work done in the nonchalant atmosphere. The late-lunch takers were dressed for work, not party. The grill was in full operation, and the drinks being cleaned off the tables were soft drinks and bottled waters rather than mixed drinks and chasers. Good food was the first hallmark of the Landing Café. The second was the nightlife. The people who visited during the day practiced a little derring-do knowing they frequented a women's restaurant/club. But the main attractions were the atmosphere and the generous preparations from the grill.

A hostess in black satin pants, white shirt, and neat bow tie escorted Tru to a cozy corner. A waitress arrived and took her order for iced tea with a straw. The café comprised two worlds, one for the day and one for the night. Tru figured a time warp lurked in some shadowed corners and would emerge after dark, and with it the wealthier lesbians of the city. The aromas of fresh breads and simmering beef wafted on the air. A quieted dance floor was covered by a brightly lit salad bar and other complementary arrangements.

As she waited for the waitress, Tru looked over the menu and decided on the Philly sandwich with salad. Having decided on what to eat, Tru took time to survey the scene and hope that she didn't see anyone she knew or would remember from her previous encounter in another darkened bar. Satisfied she was safe or suffering from a delightful case of amnesia, Tru settled back and rummaged through her briefcase for the reports.

The waitress appeared and took her order. Pulling out the papers and leaning forward to more closely study the photographs of the remains of the people and the explosive devices, Tru allowed herself one of her ten daily cigarettes. She was trying to cut back on everything. She had been drinking too much and smoking too much after she left Eleanor. She knew she might feel like death warmed over, but she wasn't going to kill herself for effect. Not anymore.

Long minutes later, Tru looked up when she thought the waitress was bringing her food. But it was the hostess escorting another late-afternoon diner. Tru's eyes were unable to adjust from the glow of the table lamp's glare on her papers. She nodded in what she thought was the general direction of the hostess and the guest to dispel any suggestion of staring. They made their way past her without comment as Tru saw the waitress heading toward her with her lunch.

Marki watched Tru lean over the papers and folders on her table. She couldn't believe her luck. She'd almost gone back to her office. What muse or angel kept her here sipping on soda until that woman arrived? Tru hadn't seen her sitting in the dim light. Lady Luck had smiled when the hostess seated Tru directly across from her. Marki watched the intensity of concentration steal across Tru's face and make her forehead furrow. Cute. She seemed so intense and lost in her work. Marki could not take her eyes from her. Intriguing, she thought. This appeared to be a different person from the one she'd seen, touched, and aroused last week. This was a woman serious about her job or whatever she had in front of her.

Marki wondered what it was she did for a living and tried to guess. It wasn't an easy task. Marki speculated about her being a salesperson adding up her accounts, a bureaucrat, or a student. She whimsically wondered at the notion that she might be a secret-agent courier for the government. Whatever she was and whatever she was doing, Marki figured the greatest danger she might currently face was the likelihood she'd spill tea on the work she bent over so intently.

Marki's eyes followed Tru's every gesture, but her gestures provided no clues about the woman who made them. Tru's clothes didn't help Marki come to any decisions either. The jacket was well made and matched her slacks. A pastel blouse fell gently open at her neck, revealing the glint of a small gold chain. Her hair was expertly cut, but every now and again a worried wisp of hair fell between Tru and her work. There appeared to be gentleness about her even as she attacked her work in a no-nonsense manner. These few new dimensions were appealing to Marki.

Marki found herself intrigued by the absent way Tru's hand lifted the persistent strand of hair back and away from her face. There was no rush or waste in the motion. It suited her, Marki thought. The action seemed incongruous for the woman she'd ravished at the bar. This woman bespoke poise as well as the quietly held grief she had heard her speak of to George.

There were contradictions at work here. The woman Marki stared at was not quite what she seemed. As a psychologist, Marki wondered if the mixed signals were a sign of an unstable personality or a momentary unstableness in the woman's life. Marki laughed at herself. Unstable. Marki chuckled and wondered how many of her colleagues would consider her unstable if they knew she occasionally worked as a bouncer in a women's bar because she wanted to relive the memories of her college days?

Unstable? Maybe. Maybe not. One thing for sure, Marki thought, Tru was an exciting woman. The first woman in some time who gave Marki something else to think about besides the publish-or-perish world of the university. Unstable? Hope not, Marki prayed. Graduate students were unstable. She was constantly surrounded by them. They were crazed with worries about grades and proper manners of genuflecting and kissing up to professors. There were also a few seriously psychotic candidates. Some of those always managed to get in and stay in the field of psychology. Stranger still were the psychology department groupies from other disciplines who filtered in and out hoping to learn enough to cure or curse themselves. The worst were the law students. They were always scrutinizing every move and gesture in psychology so they might use it against their competitors in some future criminal court case.

Another professor would be a different and more certain kind of hell. She'd been through that with Marleen. Their separate careers had separated once and for all when Marki had been offered the department's chair with the University of Missouri at Kansas City. Tears and recriminations had left Marleen in San Jose. Desire for academic upward mobility brought Marki to Missouri. It had been a great career decision but not the best personal choice she'd ever made.

Marki watched Tru and hoped she was more than an intriguing creature who'd fallen into her arms some nights ago. Tru appeared to Marki to have a career in the real world outside academia, the real world Marki had lost contact with years ago during graduate school days. Watching her, Marki noticed that Tru appeared to work hard for her living. Marki's world was dominated by jurying journals, refereeing contests of will between competitive professors, or fending off fawning graduate students. Unstable or not, this woman looked as though she could and would handle herself out in the world. At least as long as it didn't battle her too often to her knees.

Marki shuddered in sweet reflection at the

memory of their evening. Marki knew she'd taken advantage of a situation. She hadn't known the circumstances that had thrown Tru into her arms, but the feel of the woman had enticed her, excited her, and caused her to revert to the sensuous, predaceous behavior she was prone to. The feel of the woman and the climax she'd shared had shattered Marki's carefully constructed cloak of composure. It was true, like her name. Tru had struck deep and full into Marki's neglected desires. It had been a renewing experience, and Marki wanted more. She wanted more of the woman and the cravings Tru hid in her all-business suit.

Marki wondered how best to pursue the creature she saw sitting across from her. She'd known desire and need before. She'd known love too and wanted it again. She sipped her drink. She wanted to meet the true in Tru. To know her and in doing so to let Tru know her. There had to be a way, she affirmed to herself. There had to be a way that would not frighten, alarm, or cause Tru to run for the first available exit again.

"I want to know you, have you, and hold you," Marki whispered across the distance to Tru. "I want you again."

He knew hate. It was all he was capable of feeling. Hate and the need for control. He was in control; there was nothing anyone could do to stop him. They were stupid. He could see them, but there was no way they could see him.

He felt the power running through his fingers and

up along his arms. It made his shoulders tingle and his head vibrate. This was the best of it. This is what made it real.

The band saw sang as he guided the wood through its turns. He loved the feel of wood, the warm, live vibrations and the veins of growth running through it. Once wood had been the greatest part of his pleasure. But for the last year he had known it simply as a tool to quench his hate. The broad band sander smoothed the unfinished edges and raw surface to an even, silky finish.

He would take his time. Time was all he had. There were lots of bastards out there, and they weren't going any place. They didn't know he was coming for them. It would be one at a time. Everything that lived was either predator or prey. He knew he was providing a necessary balance to the universe. He was part of a greater plan. He could pick them off like the dumb grazing beasts they were. They wouldn't miss each other as he lined them up for the kill. They wouldn't know. But the thought made him sad. They wouldn't know what was happening or why. He was so clever they might never understand the real power of his genius. He felt resigned to his fate. He was an artist, and it was all too often the lot of an artist to go unheralded, unappreciated, and alone. It was a burden he would bear and the cross he would carry. He would do it for the sake of art and for Marie. He could bear any burden for Marie.

Chapter 7

By late Thursday evening Tru had spent several days in the federal building haggling and hassling with the local FBI agents. It had been as frustrating, pointless, and obtuse as her visit with Detective Quire. The only real difference between the sessions was that she had enjoyed Quire and his sarcastic approach. In the FBI she'd found that arrogance and smugness were the main stays.

In assisting local law enforcement with the two bombings, the FBI had performed the technical examinations. The fact that both packages came through the postal service had put the FBI and the treasury department on the case. Each government unit had performed an analysis. It had taken weeks. The FBI and treasury department had argued jurisdiction with each other. Finally, the justice department stepped in and made them share with each other. Their attitude with Tru seemed to suggest that the agencies were still smarting from the rebuke.

Obligingly but with a lot of condescending authority in their tone, they guided Tru through the lab reports of the remnants of the explosions. Even though the bombs had straddled state boundaries, the federal government was not interested in following up the cases. It didn't matter. They could find no connection or relationship between the two events, no connections between the two victims. The only available thread linking them was the homemade plastique and the finality of harm. The glimmer of hope Tru had felt when she walked into their labs had quickly vanished.

Regional bank robberies, extortion, gang related violence, far-right extremists, planned parenting office murders and mob business enterprises were the foci of investigations that kept their plates full. The FBI and treasury department had all they could do to keep track of their own efforts and court preparations. Cutbacks in government and downsizing of field agent staff took a big bite out of their limited budgets.

Tru wondered if the whole world was frustrated, anxious, overworked, and pushed to the brink. It was uncomfortable business for everyone. Pushed and forced toward demands that stretched people beyond their effective ability made for surly associates and associations. Tru didn't like the way the nineteen-nineties were shaping up for anyone. Millennium fever and fear of the future seemed to have everyone collapsing into hard little shells. The world, which seemed to be a little meaner and a little less gracious, it was tugging at Tru to give in to the downward spiral.

The feds did oblige her enough to let her have photocopies of lab reports and copies of the photographs of the exploded packages. It was little enough before they sent her on her way. Her briefcase latches stretched under the added pressure of the new documents. So did Tru. As she left the building, they took back her visitor's badge and waved her out into the darkening March sky.

Driving south on Broadway Tru's inner voice nagged at her. Nothing felt right. She couldn't get a sense of the victims, the bomber, or anything that might connect them. She was adrift on a sea of technical detail and best guesses from a variety of self-espoused experts. It wasn't that she didn't trust their judgment. There was no judgment, just facts. Cold, hard, lifeless facts making her briefcase and mind buckle under the minutia.

As she drove, she flipped open the briefcase. The hinge sprung open in a small explosion and sent papers tumbling to the floor on the passenger side of the car. Tru grabbed at the briefcase and papers fell out. She gave up in exasperation and rummaged through the remaining packet. She felt a key, the key to Donald Southwick's house. She had pilfered it from the police department's property unit in the downtown headquarters late the day before. It had been a whim. But now, with nothing and nowhere else to turn, it seemed like the best, if not only, course of action available.

Donald Southwick had moved into his parents' home on Ward Parkway two years ago. He'd arrived from his more bohemian quarters in the gallery he'd owned in the West Port district shortly after his mother died. His father had died twelve years ago, but not before he had made a fortune investing in the greeting card business along with a few suspiciously lucky blue-chip investments. Southwick's house was pure Ward Parkway. A grand neo-Tudor, expansive green rolling lawns, carriage house-cum-guest quarters, fancy backyard hedges, and a tendency toward English-garden sentimentalities. The wide curving driveway was partially hidden from the street by trees, shrubs, and manicured flower beds.

Tru looked at the rambling peaked roof, the balconied bedroom windows, and the darkened front door. The estate looked massive, and she knew it was from the descriptions provided by the bomb squad. They'd been all over the grounds, rooms, cubbyholes, guest house, gardens, and drawers in the place months ago. The only thing they'd found of consequence was a very dead Southwick in his library.

Tru thought that if Southwick had any last thoughts he might have been deeply disappointed that he would never again be able to look out on the neat and tightly maintained garden, never again be able to sit with his back to the arched bay windows and let the sun slide warmly across his shoulders while reading at his desk, never again get to stand in front of the fireplace on a cold night and watch the snow fall soundlessly to the ground. Or not. Maybe he knew what he had. He simply didn't have it for very long.

Tru sat in the car absently twirling the key chain with its solitary key to the Southwick house. The house had been closed for months, and she found herself faintly reluctant to enter something that looked like a mausoleum. She wasn't superstitious or afraid of the dark; she didn't believe in ghosts or things that went bump in the night. Well, some things that went bump in the night were bad guys, and she respected that sort of dangerous potential. Still, she felt a tingle of nerves race up her back and had to shake it away before she steeled herself to get out of the car.

Using the steel encased flashlight, Tru located the lock and twisted the key to open the door. Once inside she shut the door. The sound of the latch catching rang like a shot in the marble foyer. Tru was a little surprised at the sound of the door. Her imagination had kicked into overdrive. It didn't make her happy, but there was nothing to do about it now. She was in and determined to go through with her own search of the premises.

Sweeping the entrance, she felt for the light switches on the ornate glass-and-wood doorway. She turned on the lights, but their glare made her slap them off. She didn't want the local private security agency jumping up and down on her if they caught her wandering around the house. She hoped Southwick's neighbors were no more mindful of one another's business than those in her own apartment building. She wondered what the chances of that would be in a neighborhood where nothing bad was ever supposed to happen to all the 'really nice people.' Sniffing at the goose bumps rising on her arms, Tru walked down the hallway toward the library.

At the sight of the open library door she cut off the flashlight. A three-quarter moon flooded bright rays through the windows on the south and west. It was lovely on the walls of the room. Tru turned and snugly pulled the huge pocket doors together. She walked slowly and carefully, trying not to trip over unexpected furniture or the free edges of the large Oriental rug that covered the floor. At the windows, Tru reached up and drew shut the heavy brocade curtains. As she pulled the last one closed, the room was plunged into blackness. The only sound inside the house was her breathing. She switched on her flashlight. She found a lamp near a chair and another small light over the desk where Donald Southwick had drawn his last breath. The soft small lights brightened the corners of the room. With her flashlight for detail, Tru stood less of a chance of alarming neighbors or creating the unpleasant opportunity of having to confront quick-draw private security force who patrolled the Ward Parkway homes.

The room was cool, and Tru caught the faint odor of industrial cleaning detergents. The detergent and balm fragrances were definitely present. The sticky-sweet smell of Southwick's blood and brain would have been eliminated by the cleaning crews. They had been hired by distant relatives immediately after the police had returned the care of the house to them.

Two-thirds of the room's wall space was covered

by built-in polished walnut bookcases that stretched upward to within three feet of the ceiling. Above the bookcases sufficient space was left for the placement of large dead animal heads with glazed eyes and of fish mounted on polished plaques. Tru stared at the masculine regalia in disdain. The books drew Tru's eyes. They were book bindery works of art. Three-, five-, and seven-ring spines were covered in black, burgundy, blood red, or muted gray leather. They were lined up by their respective topics. She let her feet be drawn to the shelves and gazed with envy at the collection of fine works and finely wrought bindings. She reached up and drew a book off the second shelf. It was the first in a ten-volume series of Myths and Sacred Objects. The leather seemed to warm quickly in her hands and she opened the volume to find marbled endpapers. To her surprise, the pages cracked and crumbled under her fingers. Tru replaced the book and went along the shelves testing one book after another. The results were all the same.

"Mr. Southwick," Tru said softly into the room, her voice incredulous, "you had this wonderful library, fit for a king. But it was just part of a decorator's design. Very impressive books, unopened, unused, an impression. Shame on you."

Tru walked away from the rows of books on the wall and back to the desk where Southwick had met his end. It had been a beautiful piece of furniture. Had been. The deep scar and shattered top of the polished mahogany had received the same killing blow as Southwick. The office chair was missing. Tru assumed the blast that had ruined the delicate and fine features of Southwick had propelled blood and bone into the fabric. The chair had most likely been taken away by the cleaners and trashed.

Tru riffled through the unlocked desk and drew out the contents one drawer at a time. Bills, letters received, notes to himself, quick sketches of future works, and a middle drawer filled with a jumble of pens, clips, and rubber bands. Nothing unusual. Cordial letters from friends provided no insight into the late Southwick. Nothing of interest held her in the library. He didn't live in the library. It was a showpiece for after dinner drinks and an occasional firelit evening with perhaps an occasional seduction. It was decoration and nothing more.

Tru spent several hours wandering through the various rooms of the house. Donald's bedroom, although nicely appointed and decorated, befitted the effortlessly purchased look of old money. It spoke less of him than the library had. Tru began to wonder why he hadn't managed to put the stamp of his own personality on the house during the last two years of his life.

Tru was surprised. The man had been an artist, and she couldn't find anything that hinted or suggested the life or mind of an artist. She wanted the smell of oils and ink stains, the light and feel of creativity. There was none of it in the house. The house was awash with good taste, but it could have been the property of any moneyed merchant living on the parkway. It was corporate and proper. She wondered how art could have ever sprung from such blandness.

"Too many old movies or too many stereotypes working in my head," Tru argued aloud at the empty house.

Huffing her disappointment, she walked through the stainless steel kitchen and out the back door. Across a short expanse of asphalt, the large converted carriage house stood against a backdrop of towering evergreens. The moon caught and held the northeast section of the carriage house in bright relief, making a stark contrast of light and shadow. The building looked like a slice of a whole, as if only half a building existed in this world while the other half was caught in a lost dimension.

The building's side door was unlocked. That peculiarity bothered Tru, and she unsnapped her gun as she opened the door. Tru stepped over the three-inch door guard into the garage and carefully moved against the wall. Holding her flashlight away from her body, she flicked the light on for a quick look. A Mercedes and a new Land Rover stood in the sudden glare. To her left a wide set of stairs traveled up toward another floor. First checking the bottom floor and the interior of the vehicles, Tru walked up the stairs to the second-floor landing.

The solid railing that lined the staircase hid the room from her until she was almost on the last step. The moon flooded the room with light. Tru quickly glanced around. Turning, her heart slammed into her chest as she saw two figures lounging against the wall to her right. Her gun came up, and in the twinkle of a millisecond she managed to stop herself and not shoot holes into the tall people painted on stretched canvases. They glared wonderingly at her through the moonlight.

"Shit, shit, shit!" Tru breathed huskily. Her hand trembled with adrenaline as it tried to return to its lower cover angle. She didn't want to embarrass herself or the department again. She'd been through it once with them before.

It had been in a department store. The officers on the scene had thought the perpetrators were believed to be inside. Tru and another officer went in while their backup stood by in case anyone got past them. She had almost gotten to the back of the store when it happened. There had been a lone figure, barely visible from the reflected glow of streetlights flooding in. The figure moved, and she'd called to it to halt and give up. A moment's hesitation. Then, as surely as she drew her own weapon up in front of her, the figure did the same. She yelled out to stop, to not risk getting killed. Instead, the figure crouched down and she saw a gun aimed at her. She hadn't remembered pulling the trigger. She'd been desperate and knew her opponent was desperate too. The sound of her gun shattered the silence, and her bullet shattered the mirror. Later, the internal affairs unit informed her that in her crouched position she'd shot herself squarely between her mirror-reflected eyes. She did offer to pay for the mirror, but the store owner had politely and amusedly rejected the offer. The department gave her two days off without pay and made her go back through firearms qualifications again.

Tru figured a repeat of the incident might earn her more than a few days off. The thought of handing Captain Rhonn her ass in the midst of the special evaluation made her forehead break out in a cold sweat.

"Ease up," she said as she tried to quiet her racing heart. She glared at the painting.

Quickly searching the remainder of the open floor, Tru reassured herself that she was alone. The floor stretched unbroken by walls or other barriers from one end to the other. The north ceiling had been largely replaced by interlocking panels of glass. Half of the red brick on the northwest wall had been replaced by square bricked glass. It was the studio and artist's workshop Tru had been unable to find in the main house.

She searched her mind but could not recall any reports referring to this building as anything other than a carriage house used by guests. But it wasn't; this was an artist's studio. The light would have been nearly perfect for work during the day. Tru felt relief after having seen the sterile environment of the house. Here was the place Donald Southwick worked and did his art. It was open. A place free to let his mind wander. This place would give her insight into Donald, whether it would be of help or not. She wouldn't have to go snooping through things at his gallery if she found what she wanted in the loft. It would save her time and give her a sense of the man whose murderer she wanted to find.

She thumbed through his papers, ran programs on his computer and studied the ideas of artwork. She checked the projects he'd left incomplete and the progress of the sales and sales potential of pieces he had been working on. Everything was as he'd left it before he had gone back to the main building.

Sitting at the computer, she printed off copies of the directories, made her choices, found an empty disk, and copied what she wanted from the hard drive. While the computer whirred and chirped on the formatted disk, Tru smoked a cigarette. Inhaling deeply, she found herself curiously pleased to discover that Donald Southwick had the soul of an artist buried under the coldness of a business entrepreneur. But it was there. She wondered if it ever made its way out of the loft and into his shop. The pieces on private display in the loft were not what she'd understood he had placed with clients.

"Everybody has secrets and secret desires," Tru said softly to the painted figures as she walked down the stairs.

Tru went home to the comforts of her own space to sort through the mess of papers she'd gathered. As she turned into the parking lot, she thought longingly of Billy's Jigger at the corner but knew she should stay away until she'd managed to get some work done. She had to fight her little inner voice as it reminded her of the barbecue ribs, Cajun food, and ice-cold beer that waited for her there. It took all her discipline to shut down the noise with a sharp internal demand for quiet. The voice faded, but not without recriminations regarding the need to sustain the mind and treat for the body.

Tru glanced at the two-bedroom walk-ups of post–World War II apartment buildings. There were five apartments in each building. She had taken one of the four available. She rented on the second floor, to challenge the probability and agility of potential burglars. The buildings sat three blocks from the University of Kansas Medical Center and normally housed med students while they worked the torturous hours of residency. Her neighbors were quiet, the type of neighbors Tru appreciated.

Tru opened the back door and walked through the small efficiency kitchen into the dining room, living room, and office space. She threw her briefcase on a table and walked toward her bedroom.

The living room was separated from the office-cum-dining room by a low wood wall with fat walnut posts supporting the ceiling. Other than the bedrooms, the whole affair was a basic shotgun approach to apartment design, an approach overly popular after the war. From the living room French doors opened out onto a small veranda which held her two lounge chairs, an old walnut table, salvaged from a garage sale, and a grill.

She'd been lucky to find the place after she left Eleanor. It had been easier than she'd hoped to find living quarters near the West Port area. Fortunately, it had been between semesters when she was apartment hunting and the graduating now-I'm-a-doctor crowd had left several apartments available in the two-block area. She liked the space. It was cozy but still gave her room to stretch out.

She'd never accumulated a lot of personal trappings. Her own furniture had been stored in a garage near the suburban house she and Eleanor had shared. The house had been Eleanor's, and Tru had always felt more like a guest. The feeling had proved to be all too accurate.

Her apartment was uncluttered. Some people might have thought of it as spartan. Tru hated clutter and resisted temptation to purchase even one more item than she knew she needed. The one luxury she gave herself were her suits. She liked nice clothes. She had conservative tastes and knew that suits fit her personality. High-dollar slacks, jackets, blouses, shirts, and accessories from the finer stores on the plaza appealed to her. She was sensible and frugal enough to have a few dark skirts. She had dresses for weddings, funerals, court appearances, and other quasiperformance situations. Button-down shirts, sweaters, jeans, and other knockabout clothes were for fun rather than the business to which she dedicated herself.

There was just enough furniture, bookcases lined with cookbooks and psychosocial tomes, chairs, and work space to suit her. The living room held the obligatory couch with two chairs and entertainment center. A lone coffee table was stacked with history journals, *Science Americana,* and *Bon Appetit* for her lounging pleasure and special interests.

She emerged from the bedroom in a pair of her favorite loose button-fly jeans, a button-down white shirt, bulky sweater, and a pair of leather-and-wool slippers. Trying not to look at the computer and worktable where the files waited, Tru walked back toward the kitchen. The idea of a little soup and sandwich appealed to her before she got back to work.

Sitting at the small dining room table, Tru flipped through her notes as she spooned her soup and munched on the sandwich. Every now and again she glanced up and found herself looking around the apartment. Something was scratching at the back of her mind but it wouldn't give clues. Her eyes searched the floor, walls, and interior of her space. She'd frown and turn back to her notes.

"What, what's the deal?" She turned around and looked back into the kitchen, wondering if someone had passed by her window. No one was there. Turning her attention back to the interior of the dining room and living room, she felt the back of her neck prickle.

"Oh," she said. Tru looked at her living environment again and saw it for the first time. She chuckled a little uncomfortably at herself. The rooms were sparse, unadorned, unflattering, and barely inhabited. It was then that Tru remembered chastising the dead Southwick for not having the decency to make his house something that would distinguish him as an individual. She'd rebuked him for his lack of character but had relented when she found it inside the carriage house.

Tru didn't own a carriage house. The apartment was all she had, and everything she had was in it. The apartment was clean and neat. But there wasn't much anyone would ever be able to guess or say about her from its appearance. It was barren of personality. She realized it wouldn't be a favorable psychoanalysis.

There had to be more to herself, more *of* herself on which to rebuild her life. She didn't want to believe she had let Eleanor take it all away. Was it Eleanor's fault or her own? Eleanor hadn't been the one who'd told her to drift along, to become what Eleanor wanted, or to let being available become her point of content.

Questions flew through her mind. Who had she been six years ago? What had become of that twenty-eight-year-old? Who was she now? Who would she be in the future? If she didn't understand or believe in her past, how could she have a future?

"I'll find me again, somewhere," Tru responded. "In the meantime, I need a shrink or a drink." Poupon rubbed against her legs and made whirring question noises. "The drink for me and maybe a shrink to help unravel this bomber's twisted mind. That'd do the trick wouldn't it?" she asked Poupon. Looking around her apartment as she carried the cat to the kitchen for a late night snack she added "Okay, and maybe a decorator to do something about this place."

Chapter 8

Dawn broke through the cool March sky. Tru stirred in her sleep. The last dream of the night swirled through her mind and reformed last week's labor. Anxiety washed over and tangled her in the bedsheets. She stepped full into the dream, as a woman appeared shrouded in mist. She walked through a door of an old mansion. It was Southwick's home grown larger. Cobwebs, dust, and faded green paint covered the interior. Tru thought everything in the house needed a new coat of paint. It was incomplete and needed work. She walked toward the shrouded woman.

The phone on her nightstand screamed a harsh electronic chime. Tru grabbed at the offending instrument. Her reluctant throat struggled to make a sound.

"Tru?" the voice at the other end called. "Tru, come on girl, wake up," the old woman's voice urged. "Are you coming over here today or not?"

"Major?" Tru asked.

"You said you were coming over."

"What time is it?" Tru tussled with the sheets as she forced herself to sit up in the bed.

"It's six-thirty. Time for all good people to be up and going. That's what time it is."

"It's Sunday, Major."

"I know that. I've been up since five."

"Major, Sunday is a day of rest." Tru looked wearily out her window into the widening pink of the sky.

"Only if you deserve it. The Lord didn't make a day of rest for folks who didn't put in their full effort during the week," she chided her.

"How do you figure I didn't work hard enough?" Tru complained.

"You catch any bad guy?"

"No, but I'm —"

"There you have it. No need to make excuses. You get dressed, have breakfast, and get over here. We'll talk about it after we put in some work." The line went dead.

"Cripes," Tru retorted as she laid the receiver back in the cradle. Nothing much had changed about Major O'Donoghue since her retirement from the university. She was a constant. Tru had met O'Donoghue when she'd been completing her bachelor's degree at the University of Missouri at Kansas City. It had been Tru's last semester and the major's last year of teaching. She admired the old woman. Now in her seventies, she was as sharp, quick of mind, and formidable as ever.

Her reputation as an administrator and innovator in law enforcement was legend. In the early seventies she had converted the two-man patrol units to single-officer vehicles. It had doubled the available coverage in the fast-growing community and created the image of safety and officer presence. It had won her national recognition for efficiency and budget control. But she hadn't stopped there. She hired two ex-military helicopter pilots, put them through the basic police course, bought helicopters, and put roving patrols in the sky for instant response. The public was thrilled. Her innovations and daring had given them some palatable relief from their rising fear of crime. But she also had made enemies. And over the years the major's enemies slowly but surely gathered about her. They were patient. They waited and schemed for their opportunity to push her out.

As the nineteen-eighties arrived, her enemies discovered their chance through the FBI's method of counting criminal offenses. There was precious little agreement between the FBI scores and the statute designations within most states. A felony theft for the FBI was a theft of fifty dollars. In Missouri a felony theft had to exceed two hundred dollars in loss. O'Donoghue counted according to the requirements of the reports by the FBI and not according to Missouri statutes. It was a legitimate process. The difference between Missouri statute indicators and the accounting techniques required by the FBI was slim. But it was enough for her enemies to bring her down.

She was charged with malfeasance and misfeasance of office — a deliberate misrepresentation of facts — which were felony offenses in Missouri. She was relieved of her office and terminated before trial by the appointing authorities whose majority had turned against her. Four long months afterward she was exonerated. The truth did have a way of shining through, but after the fact. It was too late. She had been replaced by a favorite son of the police commissioner. Being right didn't help. She never returned to her beloved department. Several months after the conclusion of the case she was hired as an associate professor in the sociology department at the University of Missouri at Kansas City to teach criminology. She remained there until her retirement.

The two had hit it off. O'Donoghue loved Tru for her audacity, quickness of mind, and attention to the field of law enforcement. Tru loved O'Donoghue for her cantankerous nature, her astuteness, the stories about the law enforcement of her youth, and the foil she provided for Tru's questions whenever she was stuck without answers in her investigations. The relationship they developed was based on mutual respect and filled a void each felt in their lives.

Tru put on a fresh pair of blue jeans, sweatshirt, and her shoes before she placed a clean set of clothes into her canvas travel bag. O'Donoghue's basement, as she recalled from earlier explorations, was a crowded, stacked jumble of storage and odd collection of junk. It was going to be a long, messy day, and

Tru did not want to wear the ruin her clothes would become any longer than absolutely necessary.

"My fault," Tru responded to herself as she asked how she'd gotten involved in helping O'Donoghue clean out the basement. She'd been after O'Donoghue for months. Tru had made the mistake one night of going to the basement and fetching a bottle of wine O'Donoghue wanted. She'd walked down the stairs into a stuffed maze of boxes, papers, file cabinets, shelving, books, and things she couldn't recognize in the faint glow of the overhead bulb. It was a catacomb of dirt, dead mice, and impossible clutter.

" 'Bout time you got here." O'Donoghue greeted Tru at the door of the ranch-style house.

"I got here in great time, what do you mean?"

"It's after eight. That's all."

Walking through the living room and heading for the coffee pot Tru flashed a grin at the Major.

"Just like the office, Major. I don't clock in 'til I have to."

"Sure, and you'll not get any promotions with that attitude," O'Donoghue said, affecting the lilt of her mother's Irish cadence.

"And just what would you promote me to?" Tru said, emerging from the kitchen with a steaming cup of hot coffee.

"Today? Why, today you'll be head janitor and scrub-about," O'Donoghue winked.

"Great, sounds just like my kind of luck too. Is that the way you treat free help?"

"Free? What's free about feeding you and letting you swill my beer?" O'Donoghue countered.

"Cheap then, I work cheap," Tru corrected. Tru descended the stairs and made her way to the back double-garage doors and wondered where to start. The enormity of the task fell over her. She wondered if the major had tried to keep everything she'd ever owned over the last seventy-two years. The boxes, file cabinets, slanting bookshelves, and mounds of rubble all had to be sorted. The list of pitch-and-saves the major had given her weighed heavily in her pocket.

She breathed in deeply trying to steel herself for the job. She coughed at the stale air as she pushed by into the sweeter smell of spring. Sighing, Tru turned back toward the mayhem of confusion and set to her solitary task. She could hear O'Donoghue trudging about in the upstairs and knew the major was attempting to bring order to the equally stuffed rooms above. Her home was filled with a profusion of preserved personal memorabilia.

This may be hopeless, Tru thought drearily, as she waded with trepidation into her task. She worked steadily for three hours. She stopped only once for a cigarette and infrequently for a drink of water from a plastic cup she'd placed on the wall of the basement driveway. She figured the few drowned spring insects picked out of the cup was preferable to a crust that might be formed on it in the interior of the garage.

At one o'clock she stood smoking her second cigarette and tried to admire the work she'd accomplished. It wasn't an easy thing to do. She'd been working at a furious pace but couldn't see any real progress. A space no more than ten feet wide mocked her efforts.

Her clothes were filthy and her hands were covered in the ancient soot of dusty corners. Her eyes blinked to wash away the dust of the room.

Why do some old people keep all this crap? Tru asked herself and shook her head perplexedly.

Grinding the cigarette butt under her foot, Tru headed back to the basement stairs. She hoped O'Donoghue had something fixed for lunch.

"Finished?" O'Donoghue called from the chair Tru had left her in when she'd gone to the basement hours earlier.

"Not yet, and maybe not this century. But I think I've made a dent," she said, standing at the top of the stairs trying to beat some of the dust and cobwebs from her clothes.

"My god, woman, you're a mess," O'Donoghue laughed at Tru as she came around the corner of the room.

"And the problem with that is?"

"Go clean up. I've got sandwiches for us," O'Donoghue said, rising from her chair and heading for the kitchen.

"About time," Tru countered and walked down the hallway to the bathroom. Inside, Tru turned the faucets on, took off the dust mask, and bent her face toward the water. She hoped the dust wouldn't cake up and clog the sink.

"So," O'Donoghue said as Tru reached for her second sandwich.

"So what?" Tru responded.

"So what's eating at you? Something is. I can tell. It's not like you being too quiet."

"Really? You calling me a chatterbox?"

"Yeah, pretty much. Except when you have a case or something else eating at you." The major smiled.

"Nice woman," Tru retorted. "What makes you think anything is going on?"

"Simple. We've been sitting here for fifteen minutes. I've had to look at the top of your head while you've stuffed your face as if it's the end of food."

"I've been working, that's all. Cleaning up that stuff downstairs wore me out."

"A lot of that stuff is important. It's history. You can't just find it anywhere. Besides, if that little bit of physical exercise wears you out, you need to spend more time at one of those fancy gyms you always go to. That's not the whole story, is it?" O'Donoghue countered and shook the bag of potato chips at Tru questioningly.

"No thanks," Tru said avoiding the real question.

"Your new captain — what's his name, Rhine? Ron? —at you again?" she asked, going to the heart of it.

"Rhonn, Captain Rhonn, and he's probably just a symptom of life in general," Tru said as she surrendered to O'Donoghue's prying. She had to surrender. O'Donoghue wouldn't give up until Tru talked.

"What's Rhonn done now?"

"Not much more than usual. This time I think he's out for blood. And failing that, I think he'd accept my badge."

"What did you ever do to this guy? You screw up a case, make him look bad, get sassy with him like you do me?" O'Donoghue dug.

"Nothing. Not a damn thing. Honestly." Tru

sighed. She wondered at it herself. "I think he's just one of those surly bastards and I'm at the top of his list right now."

"Could be," Major O'Donoghue reflected.

"I can't figure it. He seems to get his kicks out of having someone in the barrel. It's like he's not happy unless someone's in office purgatory. You know, I'm convinced if it wasn't me, it'd be someone else."

"Some people are like Rhonn, Tru. Fortunately, his sort are few and far between. I had this major I reported to almost thirty-five years ago. Just like him. He wasn't happy unless he was stirring the crap somewhere. If there wasn't legitimate crap, he'd invent it. I watched him operate for the longest time, and then one day I asked him why he did what he did. You know what he told me?"

"I can't imagine."

"He said he kept things stirred up, with people talking and looking over one another's shoulder, because as long as they were concentrating on the little stuff they couldn't cause him problems. What he meant was that crap kept their minds focused where he wanted them to be focused. He believed, and I believe too, that in that way he kept them from looking at the things he was doing or the real issues in the department. Instead, they centered on the trivia while he made points with the big boys. He controlled them, and they tumbled to the trick."

"You've got to be kidding?" Tru rebutted.

"No, I'm not. Maybe your Captain Rhonn is doing the same thing. I can't say for sure that he's as smart as the fellow I knew. And let me tell you that boy was smart. He knew what he was doing and why. It worked. He'd have made colonel too, except he was killed. A boating accident two years after I went to work for him."

"He intend to be disruptive?"

"I just said that. Look, think of it this way. It's a magician's trick. The magician tells you something's going to be happening, you don't know what. Only what's really happening isn't what he's showing you, it's in his other hand or up his sleeve. He distracts you. It's management by deception."

"You think that's what Rhonn is doing?"

"Can't say for sure. But I have seen the type before. What with everything you've told me since he came on board, I'd say he's a dead ringer for the bastard I knew," O'Donoghue said as she lit her one-a-day pipe.

"Well, trick or no trick, I've got an investigation with no leads assigned to me. He said I'm the current subject of one of his special evaluations and that how I handle this case will make or break my career."

"He got rid of that friend of yours a while back, didn't he?"

"Yeah. And now I'm the new unit leper."

"Divide and conquer. Scare the masses into turning against their own, offer up a current sacrifice, and fear will scatter them to the corners like spilled marbles. Not a great management style, but it seems to be working, doesn't it?"

"All too well."

"Tell me about the investigation you're working on. What's going on there?" O'Donoghue leaned across the table to get closer to the story she hoped Tru would tell.

"Nosy." Tru laughed at the look of intense concentration on the major's face.

"Of course, what are friends for?" O'Donoghue smiled and waved her arms expansively.

"Why not. Basically, I can't figure the guy's motivation." Tru related the incidents, victim information, and bomb construction to Major O'Donoghue.

They discussed the particulars and guesses regarding the required expertise to enable the construction of homemade plastique. They explored motivational fantasies about the bomber. They wore themselves to a point of mental exhaustion and redundancy.

"I need a clearer picture of this guy. And as much as I've loved discussing it with you, it isn't getting me anywhere very fast," Tru said, summing up the explorations.

"Allright. But you can't say we didn't have fun, can you?"

"No, I can't," Tru said and headed back to the basement.

At five-thirty when she was preparing to leave, Tru realized she'd have to drive home in her filthy clothes and was not happy. O'Donoghue didn't miss the frown on her face.

"You might need some professional help," O'Donoghue said, and she glanced out from under her eyebrows to watch Tru's response.

"Is that personal, Major?" Tru asked as she tipped a beer back and finished the lukewarm mouthful.

"You know what I mean. Talk to some shrink since you're stumped. Tell them your wild guesses. Don't forget to pay them, you know, make them get into confidentiality between client and practitioner.

They have to hold their tongue then," O'Donoghue assured Tru.

"Know any good shrinks who'd tumble to the idea?"

"Doesn't matter where you start or who you find," O'Donoghue said. "I'd recommend the university. Most of those fellows don't get out much. Any one of them would jump at the chance of getting their hands on the facts of a juicy murder, not to mention your head," O'Donoghue said as she roamed the television channels with the remote.

"I'll think about it," Tru said. In irritation she snatched the controls away from the major and punched in the numbers for the movie channel. It was the standard friendly fight for channel control. As she watched the last ten minutes of an old horror movie, Tru decided she'd call the university and locate a willing psychologist. All other avenues were blocked or closed to her. It was a long shot but worth a try.

Chapter 9

"Dr. Campbell?" Sara Keen said as she leaned around the corner of the office door. She glanced in to see how busy Marki looked. She'd been Dr. Marki Campbell's secretary for less than a year and during that time knew the good doctor's temperament could be mercurial. Not often and never personal, but occasionally Dr. Campbell's temperament was unpredictable, and Sara didn't want to be on the wrong end of the mercury.

"Yes, Sara," came the distracted response as

Marki walked along shuffling papers into separate neat stacks on a table.

"Dr. Campbell, while you were in class this morning a detective called and wanted to make an appointment."

"And?" Marki removed her loose-fitting jacket and gathered her matching skirt underneath her as she sat down in her chair. The bright green, long-sleeve blouse was warm enough in the steam-heated office. Marki preferred steam heat for its soothing effect on contemporary overstressed respiratory systems. However, the steam mechanisms were not quick to respond to abrupt weather changes. The lingering coolness of the late-March nights tended to maintain a heat in the building. The pent-up steam could only be alleviated by opening windows or disrobing as much as decorum might allow.

"I told her you had office hours from eleven to one o'clock today. She said she'd be here by eleven. Was that all right?" Sara fussed with her blouse trying to straighten the bunching up at her waist. The hours of sitting and typing sometimes had a tendency to dishevel her.

"That'll be fine. It's almost eleven now, so give me a few minutes to make sense out of these tests before you show her in." Marki returned to the stacks of papers on her desk as Sara turned to leave.

"Wait. Just who am I waiting for, and why?" Marki remembered to ask before Sara vanished around the corner.

Sara fumbled in her mind for the name. "A Detective North with the Kansas City, Missouri, police department. She wasn't very forthcoming regarding the reason. She did mention it had something to do with a case she was working on. You know how mysterious detectives can be," Sara asserted.

"No, not really," Marki responded. North, North? The name had the ring of familiarity to Marki. Then it hit her. Tru North? The woman she'd sweetly accosted at the bar? The woman she'd been fantasizing about? Was the good goddess granting a wish and bringing Tru to her?

"They're always mysterious on TV," Sara insisted.

"True to form. Is that what you're saying?" Marki smiled lightly at Sara.

"You'll have to tell me after you've talked to her," Sara suggested.

"Fine. Give me a few minutes and I'll let you know when to show her in. Okay?"

"All right."

Well, thought Marki, this could turn out to be an unexpected and wonderful surprise. She turned toward one of the two windows in her office and grinned roguishly out at the view.

Marki Campbell had been given the office two years ago when she was hired as the chair for the psychology department at the University of Missouri at Kansas City. The office sat comfortably on the second floor of an old Greek house that had been remodeled into office and classroom space. A new Greek house had been constructed through a private endowment by an ancient graduate. The remodeled space and surrounding building in which Marki sat had retained the stately woods, veneers, and charm of the original pre–World War I design. Her office was spacious without pretension. The new light-blue carpeting settled the hollowness of the former wood floors. Several floor-to-ceiling bookcases had been built into the walls, but they did not overpower the room to make Marki or her visitors feel as though they were trapped in a library. A brown leather couch, two upholstered wingback chairs and a high oak table finished the cozy ordering of the room.

On the wall space available, Marki had hung enlarged reproductions of mandalas designed by C. G. Jung during the last years of his life. Marki liked them, although she was not what any of her colleagues would call a full-fledged Jungian psychologist. She entertained his notions and the notions of von Franz, Downing, Lorde, and others with equal attention. It was not the person's method or worldview per se that interested the professional or personal side of Marki Campbell. She was interested in the usefulness and utility of the method or worldview. Marki was interested in what worked when digging into and discovering the maze of the individual psyche. Paradigm and theories aside, Marki knew she was skilled in uncovering the onionskinlike encasements covering the hearts and subconscious natures of her clients, students, friends, and other interesting parties.

It was the best office she'd had since graduation. When she'd completed her dissertation and the trials of the committee, she'd left the University of Washington and took up residence in San Jose with Marleen. The new doctor Marki Campbell took the twenty-chapter, five-hundred-page dissertation and proceeded to publish her way into the annals of respected journals. The Veterans Affairs Center near San Jose, the police department, and the state psychiatric ward for the criminally insane had provided

Dr. Campbell with all the study subjects she had needed for years.

Violence and violent behavior in men were her driving interests. Even before she underwent her own psychoanalysis, she realized that it had been her stepfather and his incomprehensible outbursts of violence toward her mother that had given Marki a compelling desire to understand violent behavior in men. During the last ten years as she distanced herself from her widowed and aging stepfather, she'd learned to accept that violence was not a homogeneous epistemology. Violence coursed through all categories, socioeconomic levels, ethnic and racial lines and was undeterred by religious affiliations, educational attainment, or public prominence. Within the types ran a full range of tiny tortures and escalating episodes. Far too often, the ignored abuse culminated in an explosive murderous event.

Marki shook her head from her reverie and wondered if Detective North would arrive on time. Based on her experience, she knew law enforcement officers possessed a sort of internal drive to be punctual. She wondered if the drive was based on a set of police academy qualifications, the rigor of case deadlines, or their mother's conditioning during arcane rituals of toilet training.

If this Detective North was the woman Tru, Marki already knew one or two things about her and speculated how invigorating it would be to get to know the detective. Exciting and interesting. She looked forward to the opportunity to meet Tru again and for the first time. Marki didn't know what chance opportunity had flung Tru into her reach, but she did know she wasn't going to let chance or Tru slip through her fingers again.

The intercom buzzed softly. "Detective North is here, Dr. Campbell."

"Good. Have her wait a moment and then bring her in," Marki responded. Expectations intensified her heartbeat. She turned toward the window and breathed slowly, hoping the flush of her face might disappear before the detective was brought in. She said a small prayer of hope to the goddess.

The door opened as Marki turned her chair back to the desk to face her guest.

"Doctor Campbell?" Tru asked.

"Yes," Marki said rising to greet her. "You must be Detective North." Marki smiled as she extended her hand to the petite detective and vowed to light a candle to the goddess in thanks.

"Yes . . ." Tru faltered. The moment Tru saw Dr. Campbell, she sensed something about her. It seemed important, but she couldn't put her finger on it. A twinge of familiarity, an acquaintanceship, or rapport. Tru wanted to shake the feeling. She had met a lot of people in her line of work, and sometimes the faces seemed blurred together when she concentrated on a case.

"How might I help you?" Marki asked as she watched a flicker of attention dance in confusion across Tru's face. She liked the clothes the detective wore to their meeting. The black double-breasted jacket with gold buttons, black slacks, black shoes, and a muted light gray blouse set off by a small scarf at her throat stated the meeting was all business. Marki appreciated that Tru's taste in clothes didn't run to the off-the-rack jumble Marki

112

knew was favored by most career law enforcement types. This woman knew her own style, had invented it, or had been coached into it by someone who understood the effect of personal presence. It was armor. Marki was reaffirmed in her desire to know all there was to know about the real Detective Tru North.

"Do you mind if I sit?"

"No, not at all. Apparently my manners are slipping. Would you like some coffee or tea? Sara could bring us some," Marki offered.

"That would be nice. Coffee, please. Black, no sugar," Tru said as she settled into one of the chairs.

Marki rang Sara and put in the request. As she hung up the phone, Marki walked around her desk to sit next to Tru.

"What would you like to talk about?" Marki said as she lowered her long-limbed body into the chair.

Tru felt the hairs go up on the back of her neck. The tone of voice Dr. Campbell used reminded Tru of the flirtatious gestures she had sometimes exercised with interesting and unsuspecting women. A little nagging sensation ran across Tru's mind but wouldn't slow down enough for Tru to see it. Tru brought herself up to her full seated height and tried to ignore the sensation.

"I have been assigned a case that's giving me fits," Tru said as she tried to get control of the interview.

"How so? And how do you think I can be of assistance?"

"Actually, I don't know. But you might. Talking to a shri . . . a psychologist was a suggestion a friend made because she thought, and I think, I need to be able to get into this guy's head to catch him before he hurts anyone else," Tru stumbled through.

Marki leaned closer across the table and started to respond to Tru as Sara walked through the door with their coffee. Marki withdrew and noticed Tru look away from her directed eye contact.

"Thank you, Sara. The detective and I will be chatting for a little longer. Please hold all calls."

"Certainly," Sara demurred, and quietly exited. She closed the door behind her.

"Where was I . . . Dr. Campbell . . ." Tru looked back into Marki's open, friendly eyes.

"You were telling me about a suspect you're trying to locate. But I don't understand why you called me. Wouldn't any shrink do?" Marki taunted.

"Right. No. I mean, I'm sorry about the shrink thing." Tru felt her face warm to a light blush.

"Not a problem, I assure you. And you blush wonderfully. Most people don't, you know, blush. At least not very readily after they've passed adolescence."

Marki watched as Tru's pupils widened in surprise. A tender detective, Marki thought. How engaging.

"I'm not sure I catch your drift," Tru lied.

"It's true. Or, at least you seem to blush fairly easily. Remember, you made a social faux pas by calling, or starting to call, me a shrink. You barely recovered in time to attempt to hide the slip in a more socially approved label. Then you blushed at your tongue slippage," Marki recounted for Tru.

"I see," Tru said slowly.

"Perhaps. Let me explain. Charles Darwin once said that human beings were the only creatures who blushed or had reason to," Marki said as she filled her coffee cup again. "Was the slip of tongue the reason for the blush, Detective North?"

"Do all psychologists play games?" Tru asked in growing discomfort.

"I'm not trying to wound your feelings, Detective, or put you on the defensive. I merely said, I found your response charming. If I had meant anything else, you certainly wouldn't be struggling to guess what it was," Marki asserted as she offered Tru more coffee.

"I see," Tru said, clearing her throat. "Actually, to get back to the issue, I didn't call you. I called the general number for the university and asked for the psych department. As it turns out, that's you. I took a chance. I was hoping to find someone available. Your secretary said your schedule was clear. When I told her I was a detective, she scheduled me into your office hours. I was hoping to either talk to you or ask you if you could point me toward someone who might help," Tru explained.

"Let's get back to your bad guy, and I'll see what I can do."

"All right," Tru said as she reached into her briefcase for her notebook. "He's a bomber. It's the way he kills. I don't know if it's by luck or design, but he seems to target one person at a time. I think he's taken out two victims, but there's nothing other than my hunch to hang that on. One victim lived here, in Kansas City, the other in Olathe on the Kansas side of the line."

"I remember reading something about those deaths," Marki said.

"They didn't both die. The guy in Olathe

survived. He doesn't have a face; he's on life support and is kept comfortable with morphine. I don't know if I'd call that living."

"Good point," Marki said as she shuddered. "What makes you think these two incidents are connected?"

"A few strings, nothing much more. The bombs were small wooden boxes, mailed locally, and each explosive apparatus used what the lab boys have figured out to be homemade plastique," Tru said as she flipped through the pages of the notebook looking for the bits and pieces that made up her investigative efforts. She knew she hadn't given Captain Rhonn an update and would need to soon or suffer the consequences.

"What is plastique, homemade or otherwise?"

Tru looked up, blinking at the question and into Marki's eyes. "Sorry. That's an explosive compound. A very little goes a long way. It has the ability to be shaped, arranged, and molded into any form the user might want. It's plasticlike. Its makeup is partially rigid but flexible enough to make it into rope, paper-thin sheets, blocks, or anything else."

"And you can make this at home?" Marki asked in astonishment.

"I certainly wouldn't try it. But yes you can if you have the formula, and are very careful and very lucky. When you start mixing the chemicals together, this stuff is highly unstable. One wrong move and you and your bathtub go up in one big blast."

"Bathtub?"

"That's a joke. Their laboratory is wherever they mix this stuff."

"I guess I was under the assumption that the

chemicals and the other materials required to make something like that were somehow controlled by the government." Marki started to wonder how safe her other presumptions of the world were.

"Some of them are. Explosive compounds manufactured for legitimate use in construction, demolition, or the military are traceable. They contain tagging devises and trace materials that would tell us where and by whom it was manufactured as well as to whom it was sold. If necessary, other transaction records accessible by the FBI would tell us where and when certain types of explosives were stolen."

"So there are extensive resources available to you?"

"Yes, but none of them work in this instance, or these two instances to be more exact," Tru reminded the psychologist. "This stuff is homemade. Everything is homemade. The materials used are not traceable because whoever made them literally started from scratch."

"He's smart and dangerous. That's not a good combination," Marki offered.

"Dangerous, for sure. Smart, or lucky, I don't know. Maybe both. He would have, according the lab reports — by the way, this is all confidential, right?" Tru remembered to ask.

"Are you wanting me to be your shrink?" Marki asked, and winked suggestively at Tru

"I . . ." Tru wondered at the wink. Tru felt the tingle at the back of her neck travel down to the pit of her stomach. What was going on here? Was the psychologist flirting?

"It's all right, Detective North. Please continue. I

promise not to breathe a word of this to anyone. But for my service or services to you, I may have to extract a price," Marki teased.

She was flirting! The alarm bells of pleasurable surprise reverberated shrilly inside Tru's head. You just never know, the little voice cheered over the protesting racket in Tru's head.

"I . . . I . . ." Tru stammered.

"Continue, Detective," Marki insisted gently.

"I, I mean, the lab reports say that the explosive base which made the nitroglycerin was created from a compound known as fuming nitric acid. Fuming nitric acid is not an explosive itself but can be when mixed with the right other compounds. The compound for nitrating, or creating an explosive agent, that was chosen by my bomber was starch. Normal, everyday, in-the-kitchen-or-laundry room starch."

"Amazing."

"That's not all. This guy had to go through about fifteen incredibly touchy procedures before he got his nitroglycerin. He'd probably already bought his nitro-cellulose, that's nitrated sawdust. He could have gotten it from any gun store in a thousand-mile radius that caters to gun enthusiasts," Tru assured the psychologist. Tru wondered if the woman had any name other than Doctor.

"Nitrated sawdust?"

"Yes, nitrated, extraordinarily finely-ground saw-dust. It's used in smokeless powder. If you're a gun or shooting enthusiast, one of the first things you learn is that buying new ammunition or reloads can be very expensive. The alternative is to buy your own reloading equipment and cut out the middle guy. It makes the financial burden a lot less for the hobbyist and competitor."

"I see," Marki said. She didn't comprehend much of the technical discourse, but she had the unpleasant realization that an incredibly dangerous and foreign world was going on outside her office door, a world more dangerous than she had ever suspected. She looked at Tru with admiration. There was the hint of danger about the detective. Marki liked the sensation. "So he made this compound and blew people up?"

"Almost. Before he could do that he had to take the nitroglycerin he'd manufactured and stabilize it into a slightly stiff plastic substance he molded to the lid of the boxes. Then he mailed them to his victims," Tru reminded her.

"Why didn't it explode on him before he mailed it, or explode at the post office, or at another time before his victim opened it? I thought you said the stuff was unstable?"

"It is, at the front end of the procedure. But once he got it to chemically commit, it simply turned itself into what would look and act like a small lump of gray dough. It was that dough he sealed to the lid of the boxes. The rest of the contraptions were made up of tiny tension-release detonators. The detonators released the explosive potentials. We think the detonators were made from wafer-thin pocket-calculator batteries and a delicate strip of metal under tension as a tiny trip-trigger with a crimped blasting cap.

"So when the poor unsuspecting bastard unwrapped his package, he'd only notice the wooden box. The box would be an unexpected gift. Most of us don't expect packages to blow up in our faces. The victims did what came naturally. They opened the box to see what was inside. Just like Pandora. Simple and final. But without the possibility of hope hiding inside."

"My goddess," Marki whispered.

"Not mine."

"Well, yes. I meant it as prayer, I assure you. You've read myths?"

"Good cops read farther than just the last homicide report, Doctor."

"Of course."

"Can you help me? Or is there someone else I should be talking to?"

"I'm not sure. I'm not sure at all. The story is fascinating, but I'm not sure this is my area of competency or proficiency. I'm much more at home with the study of individuals who focus their violent episodes on women and children. The incestuous father, the spouse-beating husband, your basic emotionally-abusing leeches and letches. That's my territory. It's what I study, write, and what I present at conventions. This is a little out of my league," Marki said. She shivered slightly, not wanting a new career avenue.

"Look, Doc, I need some help here. This case is important to me. In more ways than you might imagine. I'm a bit at the end of my tether," Tru said in exasperation. The coffee in her cup had turned cold, but she finished the few drops.

"All right," Marki said, stretching in the chair as she glanced at the clock on the wall above her desk. Its hands closed in on the last few minutes of the morning and would soon declare the lunch hour.

"Tell you what. Why don't we grab a bite to eat somewhere so I can rack my brain in comfort? There might be some things I think I can tell you about."

"You have time?" Tru brightened.

"For you, I'll make time," Marki nodded faintly at Tru.

"Great," Tru said as she hastily gathered her papers back into her briefcase. "I'll buy."

"Did they give you an expense account, Detective?"

"Not exactly, but it's the least I can do, Doc. You're giving me more than my fair share of time today," Tru offered.

"It's really my pleasure too, Detective," Marki responded as she walked over to the coatrack to fetch her jacket. "I've enjoyed talking to you. You know how psychologists can be, don't you?"

Tru shook her head. Dr. Campbell turned to look in Tru's direction as she slipped her coat over her shoulders. Tru saw and felt the psychologist's eyes travel slowly over her body.

"Psychologists can, and often do, work on several motives and several agendas at the same time. It's part of their nature and training. It's so deeply ingrained we quite often forget how else to act," Marki explained, returning to Tru's side. She noted that she was a full head taller than Tru. Marki imagined how neatly Tru would fit into her arms and how it would be to feel Tru's firm smooth skin next to hers. If she were true to her calling, Marki knew Tru would work out at a gym and have sensuous muscle definition.

"What agenda do you have in mind, Doctor?" Tru asked uncertainly.

A smile crossed Marki's lips as she noticed the blood rise and spread its glow across Tru's face again.

"Margarete . . . or Marki. I don't think we need to stand on formality here," Marki said as she took Tru gently by the elbow to guide her through the office door.

Tru felt the shock of recognition at the name. Marki! A bolt of electricity raced across her heart as Marki guided her through the waiting room, out the door, and toward the elevator.

"I have some explaining to do," Tru began. She didn't dare look up into the other woman's face.

"All in good time, my dear detective. All in good time," Marki said as they headed toward the barest possibility of lunch.

Chapter 10

"Where would you like to go?"

"What?" Tru directed her attention back to Marki, away from the forced focus she'd deliberately fixed on traffic.

"I said, where would you like to go? For lunch, that is," teased Marki.

"Hannigan's would be fine with me. You?" Tru said. Tru hadn't looked at Marki since they had left the university. It was an improbable situation, and she didn't know what to do.

"About that night at the bar," Marki began.

"Not right now. Give me a few minutes to regroup. I just can't..." *Think!* Tru snarled at herself. *I just can't think.*

"All right. I won't press. But I do think it would be better if we talk. Take your time. I'll be right here."

No doubt, Tru complained to herself. She was trapped in her car with the woman she'd let... She tried not to think. But without trying, the visual replays rose dangerously in her mind.

Hannigan's was a small, unpretentious Irish pub in West Port. The building, according to local legend, had been made of half-hewed logs, some native stone, and rich clay sod. The original Hannigan's had burned years before the Civil War. Its destruction had nothing to do with the border wars that had raged between Kansas and Missouri before and during the conflict. The fire had been the simple accident of combustion of soft rotted timbers and a red-hot stove in too close proximity.

The second Hannigan's was built in the time of the great Western movement. It had greeted the weary Easterners to victuals, supplies, and a few quick rounds of rotgut before they headed toward their futures. Hannigan's had prospered and expanded to meet the needs of the ever increasing thirsty crowds. Its two-story expanse of thick sturdy native stone walls and six-inch milled wood floors were as sturdy as the day they'd been laid.

It was not a fancy establishment. It was meant to provide a basic hot meal or rooms to enthusiastic revelers. The tables, chairs, and booths had been salvaged and maintained from a bygone era. They were functional, and periodic reupholstering made them almost comfortable. Bikers, aging yuppies, local merchants, and tourists would come to Hannigan's, rub shoulders, and generally keep out of one another's business. It was an established establishment without pretension that hid its enormous prosperity by maintaining its rustic decor.

Once inside, Tru wished she wasn't on duty so she could have a stiff drink. Then she remembered. That was how it started last time. She quickly dropped the idea. She spotted a table and nodded silently for Marki to follow her to the available space.

A bearded biker type wearing a soiled apron approached their table.

"What's your pleasure?" he asked.

"Got mine here," Marki insinuated and winked wantonly at Tru.

The biker-turned-waiter looked at Tru. Resigned to the situation, Tru smiled awkwardly at the waiter and shrugged.

"Right," he nodded. "Then perhaps something from the menu board as a chaser?"

Tru winced.

"Yes. I'll have the grilled chicken breast in the taco shell salad. Hmm, and a tall glass of iced tea too," Marki said.

"Iced tea and a Reuben."

The waiter wrote their order and wandered back to the kitchen. Tru noticed they were alone again and fidgeted uncomfortably in her chair. She looked up to find Marki watching her. Tru ordered herself to sit still. Tru had heard Major O'Donoghue mention that time could slow in a crisis and seem to stretch on into infinity. Until this predicament, Tru had thought she'd only feel that sensation in a car crash, while being shot at, or otherwise at the point of certain death. Now she understood that a crisis could come from other sources and in the blink of an eye. Or was that the wink of an eye?

"You're an interesting woman, Detective North."

"Tru. Might as well call me Tru. You're the one who said there was no need for formalities, aren't you?"

"Yes, I did. You are an interesting woman," Marki persisted.

"Maybe. Or maybe you have me mixed up with someone who doesn't exist. Could be I was an intoxicated figment of my imagination that night," Tru countered defensively.

"Perhaps. But you certainly were a substantial, sizzling bit of imaginative figment. As illusive and inebriated as you were, I'm a little hard pressed to believe some of the real you wasn't around for the action." Marki leaned forward in emphasis.

"It's fuzzy, honestly. I'd been having a hard time. Personal stuff. I got drunk and stupid. I can admit that, even if I don't like the way it sounds."

"Have you ever heard about the truth in wine?"

"You're trying to say I wanted to do that," Tru said, ignoring the old bromide. "That I wanted to be there? With you? Like that? It's what I'm like or the way I am?" Tru felt disbelief send burning gall to the back of her throat.

"Yes and no," Marki corrected. "Yes, I think you are having a hard time. I don't know what it is, what it's about, what or who did it, but you're still going through it. I can see that much in your face. I knew that when I held you that night. And yes, I think it is something difficult for you to admit. You

126

feel a need, or maybe you feel safe holding on to the image of being a tough cop. And no. No, I don't think you planned to be there with me or anyone else. It happened. Wasn't it exactly what you wanted? Looking at you, seeing you, listening to you then and today, I'd say your true nature runs to the sensual, empathic, and sentimental side of temperaments," Marki explored.

"But —"

"Let me finish," Marki continued. "To my way of thinking, there isn't anyone I can imagine I'd enjoy getting to know better than you."

"Sensual? Sentimental? I can assure you, none of those words have ever been used to describe me," Tru protested, her eyes narrowing in mocking constrictions. Cold, remote, aloof, and unresponsive. Those were the words Eleanor used for her. Tru looked at Dr. Marki Campbell and wondered if she'd gotten her degree through an offer on a matchbook cover or cereal box.

"Really? Then it's been your misfortune to hang with a lowbrow crowd, my dear Miss North."

"That's not a very nice thing to say. You don't know my friends."

"Of course not. I don't know any of the lovers you've ever had either. But I can assure you of one thing..." Marki hesitated. She didn't want to move too fast with Tru. The younger woman was skittish and suffering from wounds Marki could only imagine.

"What's that?" Tru braved.

"I suspect no one has ever gotten to the place where you live. I think if someone you'd known had ever taken the opportunity to see you, touch the real you, and love you, she would have been amazed. If that had ever happened, you wouldn't have such a need to camouflage yourself with the formality you present to the world, would you?"

"That's . . ." Tru struggled to respond to the onslaught. She stopped her attempt at protesting as the biker brought their food.

The conversation stalled until he came back with their iced teas. Tru, with her mind thrown off its normal safe gyrations, tried to concentrate on her sandwich.

Rather than push the topic, Marki sat quietly eating her meal and let Tru sort through the things she'd said. It was a type of shock therapy, Marki rebuked herself. She was using a technique normally reserved for clients who had little insurance coverage. She had learned how to help them cut to the chase. She would sit, watch, observe, and listen to the nuances, and zero in on the one or two things that were creating the most havoc in their lives. Six or eight sessions later, they wouldn't be cured but they would be on the road to a better understanding of themselves, their life savings still intact.

Marki knew why she had advanced on Tru with the procedure. It was a hard-hitting technique. The personal side of Marki wanted to be able to spend time with Tru. But the psychologist wanted Tru to be startled into opening her eyes. She wanted Tru to be able to see and begin to imagine the woman Marki surmised lay hidden under the pain she'd covered herself with. No risk, no gain, Marki thought to herself.

"All right," Tru sighed. "I take it that's your other agenda item. Is there anything else I should know about before we get back to the reason I made an appointment?"

"No. I have been thinking about it and it's really pretty straightforward, don't you think?" Marki smiled brightly at Tru.

"You're telling me you're straight?" Tru laughed.

"Hardly. A poor choice of words. It won't happen again," Marki laughed, enjoying the relief the misplay of words allowed. She liked the way Tru used it to give their conversation an opportunity for a break. It showed Marki that Tru had a sense of self but not so intense as to render her unable to laugh. It was good. Things had gotten a little intense. The pause would give them an opportunity to approach each other gently. It was avoidance too, but not a full retreat.

"For the time being, I'd really like to get back to the first item on the agenda," Tru said as she looked at her watch. It was one-fifteen. "Do you have a class or something you have to get back to?"

"No. I'm totally at your disposal for the rest of the day. Things just have a way of working out sometimes, don't they." Marki smiled at Tru. She hoped to charm Tru into a sense of comfort.

"Right. While you were discreetly psychoanalyzing me, did you spare any thoughts about my bomber?" Tru asked, coaxing Marki back toward Tru's central issue. Tru hoped for safer territory.

"Maybe. First, do you have any photographs of the box or boxes the bombs were delivered in? I'd like to see some, if I could."

"Right here. This is confidential. You're like my psychologist in this, right?"

"Yes and no."

"What do you mean?

"Yes, anything you have told or will tell me will be held in the strictest confidence. No tricks, no sliding, no halfway measures. No, because I could never be your psychologist," Marki said flatly.

"Could you run that past me again?"

"It's a creed, a professional code of conduct, and a personal code of ethics. I'll not reveal what we discuss about the case because I consider myself employed by the police department through the purchase of lunch. Is that helpful?" Marki watched as Tru nodded her head in agreement.

"Good. And I can't and won't be your psychologist because I'm interested in you on the personal, sensual, tantalizing levels. I don't sleep with my patients, make love to my clients, or probe for their deepest erotic desires. And frankly, I intend to do all three and more to you and with you."

Images of Marki holding her, of Tru caressing Marki, danced dangerously through Tru's imagination. Heat spread down past her belly.

"Lucky for me you have ethics," Tru said, trying to clear her throat from sudden dryness.

"Yes, isn't it?"

"Okay, okay," Tru stumbled, remembering she'd said she'd show Marki the pictures of the bombing remains. She reached inside her briefcase and pulled out the envelopes containing the black-and-white photographs. Tru managed to hand the envelopes across the table to Marki without visibly shaking.

"Go ahead and finish your meal. I'll just scan these for a little," Marki suggested.

Tru's head was reeling. She wasn't used to having

anyone better her at parlor games. Marki was something totally unsuspected and new. The shoe's on the wrong foot, Tru protested silently. Ever since she had come out in high school, Tru had been the acknowledged aggressor. She'd been assertive, the one who initiated the seductions and courted the women she desired. At thirty-four Tru couldn't imagine she had become a shrinking violet or had the tables turned on her. What was going on? Tru had a crazy notion she'd spoken out loud and glanced quickly up at Marki. Marki's head was bent over the photographs, and she appeared to be concentrating.

Assertive? Tru snorted. Eleanor had certainly become more verbally assertive and abusive than Tru had ever imagined a woman could be to another. Tru winced at the memories of Eleanor's outbursts and abusing philandering. Tru knew that her own flirting with the idea of jumping off a bridge hadn't been assertive. Only final.

Cripes, Tru noiselessly protested, it was all a pack of labels. Assertive, aggressive, butch, femme, passive, domineering, masculine, androgynous, sensitive, withdrawn, showy, sensuous. Labels. Politically correct, incorrect, off-base, off-centered, totally full of shit. All of it. Depending on who was playing the tune, she would be seen as someone else wanted, according to her own lights and the practiced rhythms of her own mind. It didn't matter. Labels were an invention of an era; if she didn't fit this one, she'd fit another.

"An anal retentive psychopath who by no means wants to get caught," Marki declared.

"I beg your pardon?" Tru said.

"Your bomber. He's anal retentive and psychopathic. He loves what he's doing even if we don't know why. Psychopathic because it's very likely he loves the preparation and anticipation more than he loves the deed. *Psychopath* is a word that's earning renewed respectability in the field. The reason I'm applying it to this guy is that he's focused on a type of victim. Artists with commercial leanings. They're his marks. And if I'm guessing right, who they are and what they do is the issue for him, not the killing. Their deaths are means to an end. This guy is more about the getting," Marki explained.

Tru sat back in her chair and absently waved to the bartender. She reached in her briefcase and took out a cigarette while she waited.

"He's focused. There's a reason he's picking them. You need to find the reason, but it's probably something locked tight in his head. More than likely, the reason would only make sense to him," Marki continued.

"In his head? You mean like voices?"

"No. This guy's better grounded than that, otherwise he'd blow himself up instead of other people. No, his victims offended him somehow. He hits them at home. That's very personal. So is his anger."

"I think I'll have one of your tap beers. Make sure it's not one of those watered-down light things, all right?" Tru said as she pushed a five across the table to the waiter.

"Anything for you, miss?" he said as he turned toward Marki.

"The same," she nodded.

The bartender walked away, leaving Tru staring at some middle point back of the bar. Marki flipped through the photographs. They maintained their individual reflections until the bartender brought the beers.

"All right. Let's work through this," Tru said, having absorbed the things Marki said. "Two artist types, neither one in mean financial straits, get blown up by homemade plastique from boxes mailed to them. The guy is patient and meticulous, not generally considered the signs of youth and enthusiasm. Both victims are white guys, so far, so we've got a ninety percent chance the perpetrator is too. No one learns how to make homemade bombs by reading a book, so we can guess that he's been trained or educated by a university, the military, the police or some quasimilitant group. He's a loner or has running buddies as crazy as he is. He probably has some sort of minor police record but nothing that would link him to the bombings. He's got the equipment, tools, and chemical stuff. He'd have to have room to work in. He's not very likely to be living in the city in a one-bedroom apartment.

"I don't know what his employment history might have been before he started killing people, but based on what you've suggested, I'd bet he doesn't work well with people. He's been pretty busy with his little hobby. It takes a lot of his time, so I'd say he's currently and maybe historically underemployed, unemployed, or self-employed. Not someone you'd miss if he didn't call in sick. Speaking of sick, this little problem he's having with managing his anger probably isn't a new twist in his personality. He may have a hospitalization record. That could include substance abuse," Tru said, and raised her beer at Marki, "stress disorders, or any other garden-variety personality disturbance."

"That's quite an analysis," Marki said. "Did they teach you that at the police academy?"

"No. It was in a little course the FBI gave. The rest of it comes from the readings they sent home with us. The really neat thing is it's all statistics and probabilities. I even created this little program on my computer at home. I use it to check some of the assumptions I make. But it's not a science. It's more of an art form. That's the down side. I could be shooting in the dark."

"Well, it seems to me there's a lot more light there than you might have thought." Marki smiled winningly at Tru.

"Yeah. Now all I have to do is search all those haystacks for the guy who fits the categories." Tru's shoulders dropped slightly under the enormity of the task.

"It's after three," Marki interjected. "Would you like to come to my place and let me fix you an early dinner?"

"That's an inviting idea, but I'd prefer not to rush into anything. I know that's pretty lame after . . . after the other evening, but that was then, and we're here now," Tru said slowly.

"I understand." Marki knew Tru's tone was not a rejection. "What say we make a date?"

"A date?"

"A date. I'll pick you up, we'll go to dinner, talk, and start getting to know one other."

"A date," Tru repeated.

"All you have to say is yes. And since you bought lunch, dinner would be my treat. Courting. No tricks, I promise."

"Court me," Tru said, feeling an echo chamber.

"That's the idea. We court. Get to know each other, come to understand each other. Will Friday work for you?" Marki asked as she stood.

"I think I'd like that."

"Good, I'll see you at eight. Now, why don't you drive me back to my car so I can go home?" Marki suggested.

Tru never realized she didn't give Marki her address.

Chapter 11

He whistled lightly to himself as he dragged the weathered and ruined walnut cabinet to the edge of the pickup tailgate. It had been quite a find and a bargain to boot. Ruined as it was for its original use, it still contained some fine wood. He could make use of it. It was large, old, heavy, and made with the careful craftsmanship of a vanished era. He could hardly wait to cut it down into smaller pieces and rework it in his own style.

He flicked the button on the overhead garage-door opener, got into the back of his truck, and eased his find nearer to the workbenches inside his shop. Bracing himself, and straining to keep from dropping and further damaging the ancient furniture, he lowered it gingerly to the concrete floor. Standing back and puffing from his exertions, he admired the fine quality of wood under the surface of abuse.

He pulled the truck back out into the yard and entered the workshop before lowering the garage door. He walked over to the buffet and ran his hand along the top. The surface was roughened. Water stains marked misuse and several drawers lay cock-eyed in their pockets. He had bought it at an auction for ten dollars. It had been like stealing. There was more than three square board feet of usable material in the buffet. It was more than enough for his purpose. More than enough for his need.

He knew from experience that an equal amount of new walnut would have cost him more than seventy-five dollars at the lumberyard. Maybe more for the quality of tortoise swirl that ran through the grain under his fingers. Walnut was a hard wood to work with but a pleasure of results if one were careful. He had the time, the patience, and the skill to rework the wood. It lived again beneath his fingers. It was the joy he knew. There would be no other joy after losing Marie. He would make the wood take the shape of the music boxes she had so loved. The wood would make six of the small boxes. They'd sing different songs than those Marie had played for him.

He reached for a scrap piece of half-inch by eight-inch board and a rubber mallet. The sound of a vehicle slowing at his driveway caught his ears. The vehicle sputtered down into a lower gear and scattered gravel and dirt in a tight turn as it roared toward his workshop. He could see the fat balloon front tire as it halted before the half-closed overhead door. Someone turned off the machine's engine and threw a battered motorcycle helmet to the ground.

"Hello in the shop," a young male voice called out. "You in there, Clarence?"

Exasperation swept over Clarence Berenger's face, and he laid the mallet on the old buffet. His pleasure would have to wait while he dealt with the boy.

"Sorry I'm late, Mr. Berenger, but Dad said I couldn't use the car this morning." The youthful, slow-witted countenance of Harold Tillman grinned at Clarence as he raised the garage door.

"That 'sposed to be my problem, Harold?" Berenger frowned.

"No, sir. It just took me near to three hours to get this piece of shit running. I tried to call, honest."

"I was at a sale. I expected you at seven before I left." Clarence strode by the boy, leaving him in his wake.

"Well, I, I got here as soon as I could. It, it won't happen again. I need the work, Mr. Berenger," Harold pleaded. The work Harold did for Clarence Berenger was the first real job he'd had in the year since he quit high school in the tenth grade. He was twenty. Harold had gotten tired of the abuse schooling had heaped on him since his kindergarten days. He was slow, he knew that. It had been too hard to have it thrown in his face year after year. His father had relented in his hope that his son would get a basic education and let the boy leave school to look for work.

"Then you need to act like it. Come on. Your chores are still waiting on you."

Harold shuffled dejectedly behind Clarence and headed for the house. Clarence turned and watched the boy kick clods of dirt and stones from his path as he walked. Clarence felt a sudden surge of pity. He didn't know whether to feel sorrier for Harold as a man with a child's brain or for the child trapped in a man's body.

"Look," Clarence sighed in annoyance, "I'm not mad at you. It's just that I have a lot to do, and you're the only one I have to depend on. When you don't show up or don't do what I need you to, it makes all that much more work for me."

By the time Clarence finished explaining the chores he wanted Harold to do for the day, it was after noon. The day was slipping away, and Clarence hadn't gotten to his workshop. He tried to be a patient man. Clarence knew that patient men were less careless, quieter of mind, and more at peace than those who let the minor events frustrate them.

Clarence had found his way to patience through woodworking. The laying on of hands to wood and shaping it was his pleasure. It soothed and softly stirred him and helped fix the fierce concentration of anger into a slow heat. Wood kept him passive so the anger could not swell up and consume his mind. Taking the woodworking and carpentry vocational course at the community college after returning from duty in Operation Desert Storm had been a blessing. One act of saving grace.

Marie had originally suggested the idea of getting other skills. She'd told him it might help them keep the house and property, that he'd be able to earn some money turning out pieces of cabinet works from his little shop. It made sense to both of them. He could work and do a little piece or project for other folks without having to leave home.

But even with Marie helping out, they'd had many lean months. Her job as a secretary in Kansas City barely supported them. It hadn't been great, but they had managed. Twelve months later, when he'd completed the course work as a certified journeyman, things began to look hopeful. Then Marie had gotten a better offer. They thought they might be able to get their heads above water. It hadn't turned out that way. It had been a false hope. A different beginning and the end of everything.

Clarence walked back to the workshop. Clarence touched the reverse switch on the garage door and let it close out the afternoon light.

Late that evening, a little over five miles away from the heart of the West Port district, Clarence pulled up in front of Rusty's All-Rite Diner in his battered three-quarter-ton pickup. As he stepped down on the running board and slammed the door behind him, the whining tires of trucks hissed their noxious rhythms under the overpass a scant half block from the diner's door. The smell of diesel fumes, worn rubber, and spring mixed curiously in the air. He clutched the rolled-up magazine in his right hand like a weapon, and he walked toward the beckoning door.

The lights of the diner glared cheerfully to him in the roadside parking lot. He had worked a long day. It was supper time, and he was later than usual.

There were few trucks in the lot. Too late for the dinner crowd, and too early for the revelers who appeared after the bars closed. He wouldn't get much conversation. He had hoped to see a few of the tradesmen he knew, but they'd be home by now with their families.

Clarence was happy. He'd found what he'd been looking for in the recent edition of *K.C.'s Entrepreneur Monthly*. That made everything just fine.

"Well, look what the cat drug in."

"Don't start with me, Mary Beth." Clarence returned the requisite smiling threat.

"Don't start with you? Now isn't that a fine howdy-do," Mary Beth huffed at him, winking in the general direction of the three men sitting alone. Each had his own booth.

They'd raised their heads to watch Mary Beth assault the latest late-night diner. Clarence nodded toward the three in general acceptance and resignation.

"Seriously now, boys, doesn't he look just like something the cat drug in? At least right after it coughed him up again?" Mary Beth continued her tirade as she glided over to his table with a glass of water and a menu. Her dishwater-blonde hair had fallen in loose wisps about her face and framed the round, reddened cheeks of the plump woman. Her uniform was a legend of her day doing double duty as waitress and busboy. But she could serve up the meals, whisk off the spattered remains, and have the tabletops sparkling for new guests faster than anyone else in seven states.

"Now, Mary Beth, I'm a working man, and working men have a tendency to get a little gritty looking," Clarence countered cheerfully.

"Yeah, 'spose that might be right, but some people have the decency to clean up before they go out. Or have you forgotten that?" Mary Beth took Clarence's order for chicken-fried steak with gravy, hash browns, green beans, and coffee.

"This isn't the Waldorf, Mary Beth. Town's more than a mile down the service road from here. This is just a little taste of paradise in lovely Misery," Clarence winked up at Mary Beth. It had the effect Clarence had hoped.

Mary Beth blushed deeply, and her plump lips parted in exaggerated exasperation. She knew how to dish out harassment to her favorite customers, but she never knew what to do when Clarence turned the tables on her.

"That's Missouri to you foreign boys," Mary Beth said over her shoulder as she swung her hips and flounced back toward the kitchen with his order.

"Foreigner?" A man in the closest booth turned to eye Clarence suspiciously.

"Yeah, means I came from over in Kansas about ten years ago. You're considered a foreigner in these parts for at least the first thirty years. Up 'til then, the locals consider you rootless." Clarence leveled his gaze at the man. He could tell the other fellow was a trucker. The type of guy whose beefy hands signaled that the reddish complexion traveled all the way up his arms to his ruddy red neck. "Been a regular here since I quit school at the institute."

"Oh." The man grunted and nodded, satisfied.

"Our Clarence is an artist. Going to be famous

some day too. Tell the man, Clarence," Mary Beth urged.

"Leave it alone, Mary Beth," Clarence grumbled in annoyance. Remembrance drew his face into a pucker and narrowed his eyes on Mary Beth.

Mary Beth shuddered under the wilting gaze. Hell of a burr under his saddle tonight, she thought, and she hurried back to her coffee-pouring rounds.

Clarence turned his attention to the magazine he'd brought into the diner. He read the article again. He felt his palms sweat as he looked into the still and confident eyes of David Haeres. The photograph and full-page glossy layout of the article declared Haeres the best, brightest, and hottest artist in town.

Clarence turned the magazine facedown when Mary Beth brought his order. Mary Beth watched him as he dug into the gravy-covered chicken-fried steak. She liked his enthusiasm for eating.

"You're working again? This one going to last?" Mary Beth asked solicitously.

"Maybe for a little while. I'm back on with Reiling's group. They've got more work than their full-time folks can handle. Pay's always been pretty good too."

"Good for you. Hope it works out this time."

"It will 'long as I don't have some supervisor who thinks he's King Kong," Clarence said, remembering his previous encounter with a supervisor over tardiness last fall.

"You have to work at getting along, Clarence. We all do," Mary Beth said quietly to him as she walked back to the counter. "How's your woodshop work doing? Sell any more?" she asked as she picked up a wet cloth to wipe the film off the coffee machine. She liked Clarence as much as she liked any of her regulars. She wanted to get back on his good side. She depended on tips to make up for the paltry minimum wage she earned at Rusty's. If Clarence was working again, she figured he might feel generous enough to share.

"Mary Beth, are you in the habit of poking sticks at snakes?" Clarence cautioned her, and shoved another mouthful of potatoes into his mouth.

"No," she said quietly.

"I promise if anything interesting happens again, I'll let you know. Okay?"

"Sure," she replied and walked back to what she hoped was a friendlier side of the diner.

Clarence turned the magazine over and began reading the article again. A grin spread menacingly across his face. He didn't know if he agreed with the article that said Mr. David Haeres was the hottest new artist in Kansas City, Missouri, or not. He did know that Haeres would soon be the deadest. He felt good. He'd forgive Mary Beth and leave her a dollar tonight.

Chapter 12

Carla Brighton walk-skipped with the energy and enthusiasm reserved for clear, bright-eyed young women. She didn't mind that she was a glorified gofer, sent here and there to transport, carry, deliver, and round up whatever the job crews or her boss, Mr. Bill Reiling, needed. Getting the job when her father disowned her, after finding Martha's love letters, had been goddess sent.

Reiling Brothers Restoration was one of the largest janitorial and disaster clean-up companies in the Kansas City area. But Carla didn't care about

145

their profit margin. What mattered to her was that Bill Reiling let her work her hours and take off in the middle of the day for classes at the university. In two more years she'd complete her degree in anthropology and start the master's program. They job had made it possible for her and Martha to move in together. They had promised to have and hold each other forever. Life was sweet.

It was Wednesday morning, hump day, and the busiest time of the week. Billings to be mailed, shipping to be prepared, supplies to be picked up and inventoried into the warehouse. Carla dashed back inside and ricocheted through the offices, sweeping mailers, boxes, packages, and supply slips off the desks and into her quickly overloaded arms. With her white visor holding back the flow of black hair and red windbreaker clinging precariously across her shoulders, she looked like a jockey late for the horses. She dashed out into the parking lot. Packages and papers spilled from her arms as she dumped them into the tiny blue truck's bed. She frowned, realizing she'd have to re-sort them later.

Carla shoved her hand into a pocket of her blue jeans and searched for the keys to the truck. She found them and fifty cents in change. Looking at the quarters, she decided it might be a long thirsty drive around town and ran back inside to get her morning supply of cold caffeine from the pop machine.

Carla didn't notice the man disengage himself from the group of milling day-workers and move toward her truck. No one in that crowd would remember he had tossed something into the truck's bed, or had bent to tie his shoe and then wandered aimlessly back to wait with them. The van driver would come along shortly to take them to their job sites. The drifters, work-furloughed prisoners, dropouts, and aimless hard-luck types had their own business to attend to. They worked at not noticing one another, at not making contact or superficial inquiries. Their lives had taught them that involvement didn't pay well. Their only resource was the anonymity that made them part of the landscape, inconspicuous to the authorities and anyone else.

Bounding back to the truck, Carla opened the door and began scooping up the array of papers, packages, and miscellaneous debris she'd unceremoniously dumped in the tiny bed. Wind gusts grabbed at the articles as she tried to corral them in her hands. In exasperation she set a smaller package on the roof of the cab to hold down the flighty documents and gathered others in her arms as she jumped triumphantly into the driver's seat.

She started the truck and backed up. She was eager to run her rounds of the morning. The forgotten package and papers on the cab roof slid off and landed on the ground where they met the crushing impact of the truck's front tire.

The horrendous explosion peeled the wheel from its rim and viciously bucked the tiny truck into the air. Gravity sharply returned it to the pavement. The men who had been waiting for the van scattered like windblown leaves. Secretaries, bookkeepers, and both Reiling brothers poured out into the parking lot in time to see the smoking cab interior disgorge Carla onto the bruising asphalt. She crawled, struggled, and rolled away from the truck. The startled employees hesitated and then rushed to her aid.

Tru arrived as the ambulance pulled away from the Reiling Brothers Restoration parking lot. It was a confusion of ambulances, fire trucks, EMT vehicles, city utility trucks, patrol cars, and unmarked units. Police officers and firefighters had apparently competed in cordoning off the area. A wide looping circle separated the ruined truck from the crowd as it sat forlornly in the midst of bright yellow ribbon. Black letters of CRIME SCENE: DO NOT CROSS and the vibrant reds and black of the fire department's FIRE INVESTIGATION: DO NOT ENTER vied for equal attention. Patrol officers struggled to restrain reporters, curious onlookers, and potential witnesses away from the scene and one another.

Tru avoided the main crush of bodies and walked through the maze of firehoses, gawkers, barricades, streamers, and electrical cords toward the ruined truck.

"What happened, Bob?" she asked and looked up at the large detective she stopped next to. From the time he was a rookie patrolman, Bob Jones had been dubbed Lurch by his fellow officers. At six-foot-four and tipping the scales at three hundred and twenty pounds, he'd earned the name. He didn't have a mean, spiteful, or vicious bone in his body. But he was a huge mischievous practical joker.

"Tru, old girl! What brings you out this fine morning?" he beamed cheerfully at her. For all his lumbering, good-natured style, Tru knew Jones to be one of the finest investigators in the state. His natural buoyancy could keep afloat conversations, investigators and their perspectives on the befuddlements of life.

"Stop with that old stuff. Talk to me. Do you think this is my bomber's doings?"

"Might be. Come here," he said as a huge hand clamped on her shoulder and guided her to the remains of the truck. "Amazingly, the girl driving that truck didn't die. Seems the concussion was wasted on the tire. The firewall protected her from any metal projectiles," he said as he pointed along the peeled fender and exposed engine compartment. The windshield had sustained some of the impact and had been transformed into a maze of shatter-resistant webbing.

"She's alive?" Tru asked in astonishment. Artists and delivery trucks? It didn't make sense to Tru.

"Yes, alive. But not really altogether all right. She's got one hell of a headache, maybe a concussion. The medics were concerned about permanent loss of hearing. She was almost sitting on top of that thing when it went off. It's a wonder she and the truck didn't just go up in flames."

"Lucky lady," Tru whistled under her breath. "Where'd they take her?"

"Troost General. She was unconscious when I got here. She's not going anyplace else for a while. Is this your case, you think?"

"If Rhonn has anything to say about it, and if it's got a connection to the guy I'm looking for, probably," Tru said as she surveyed the scene.

"No skin off my nose. But this one doesn't fit him, does it?"

"I don't know. First sight says no," Tru sighed. "However, it's too early to tell, isn't it?" She pulled a notebook from her pocket.

"Well, let's try not to get in each other's way. I think I can take you in two out of three falls." Bob tapped her playfully on the shoulder with a fisted ham hand. The tap sent Tru staggering. "Sorry," he called as his deep voice guffawed cheerfully.

"Touch me again, Bob Jones, and we're engaged," she warned. She tried to match his playful bravado and mask the bruising her shoulder had suffered. "The man's dangerous," she muttered as she sketched her first perspective of the scene.

"By the way," Tru said, maintaining her distance from Jones, "what happened to the wheel?"

"Hell, it was skinned off that axle like a rotten grape. Flew twenty feet and crashed into the back of another of the Reiling guys' vehicles. It's resting on the ground near the van over there," Bob obliged.

Tru saw the flattened tire still partially clinging to the bent rim and made a mental note to look at it later. She was more interested in the remains of the exploding package and told the evidence technicians to send her copies of their reports. She returned to her car and retrieved a tiny Nikon camera. Tru looped the long leather thong of the camera over her neck. She wanted to have it available to take photographs when the mood struck her. She walked back around and through the crime scene.

An hour later Tru had half a notebook filled with stories from Reiling Brothers employees, five sketches of the area, and major points of evidence location. She had requested the police photographer to take several shots she wanted to highlight, and had asked for a list of all the employees the Reiling Brothers had hired over the last two years. Mentally checking off a list of proper procedures, she retraced her steps and walked around the perimeter again.

The gawking crowds had spilled over into the street and stood around in tight bundles at the vehicles of late media arrivals. The TV crews held court in various locations around the protected perimeter. The local television personalities amassed the largest numbers of fans, while the radio broadcasters' vans suffered from neglect.

Tru stood in perplexed amazement as she watched the spectacle from her vantage point near the ruined truck. It never ceased to amaze her. Violence held an incredible fascination for people. The gawkers and sightseers of disaster offended her sense of propriety. It seemed as though mayhem and catastrophe held a lot of people's attention longer than love ever could. She knew if given a choice, she would choose to wander on some remote shore far from annoying crowds. In a fit of piqued revenge she raised her tiny camera and snapped randomly at the huddled, rubbernecking simpletons.

The evidence technician had sketched and photographed the flight path of the mangled tire and had tagged it for evidentiary recovery. Tru walked to where it lay and crouched down to get a closer look.

"Can I move this?" she yelled across the lot to Bob Jones. He was talking to two evidence technicians.

"Yeah. We've done everything to it we can except pack it up and carry it home."

Tru picked up what was left of the tire and rim. The sooty black rubber smudged her hands as she stood up to balance it. Bending over, she examined the area of contact with the bomb. The concussion had stripped away half the rubber and steel-corded tread. Some of the components had been jammed up inside the tire. She reached into the collapsed cavern and felt along the smooth interior walls. Just before she lost her elbow to the gaping maw of the tire, her fingertips touched something that felt like a dried leaf. Tires aren't stuffed with leaves, her inner voice tickled at her. Yes, they are, when they get blown into them, she hushed at the voice.

Slowly and carefully she grabbed an available edge of the material and drew the object out of the tire. A brittle piece of brown wrapping paper smudged by fire came into view. She stood motionless and marveled at the ragged piece of charred paper. Clumsily scrawled lettering addressed the remaining piece of package.

"Bob," she whispered. Her throat suddenly constricted. "Bob!"

Tru gestured vigorously with her head as she motioned for him to come to her. She was afraid that if she moved, touched it less gently, or even sneezed, it would disintegrate before her eyes.

"What's the fuss?" Bob asked impatiently as he strolled to her side.

"Does this look like a packaging label to you?" Tru grinned broadly up at him.

"Christ on a crutch," Bob exclaimed as he waved the techs over.

"No one on a crutch. But someone we need to meet," Tru said. The technician held open the small plastic evidence bag as she dropped the label into it.

"Of all the fucking, stupid . . ." Clarence screamed and sputtered over the ear-shattering music as he gunned his truck across the Paseo Bridge. "You moron!" he shrieked. Tears of frustration and terror welled in his eyes. The image of the petite detective moving through the parking lot replayed itself in his mind. He'd stood near the blast site entertaining himself. He'd been watching the police fumble and stumble over themselves. It had been a circus, and the police were the clowns. But he waited too long. He'd lingered, reveling in the ringmaster's power he held over the scurrying minions of the law.

The inexplicable detonation of the package had panicked him and sent him hurrying away with the tangle of panicked laborers. He had managed to reach the safely of his truck and find the half-empty pint of scotch in the glove compartment. Two long drafts on the wood-cured pleasure had helped him to bring his anxiety under control.

Crowds had poured out of the buildings in the industrial park, traffic had swerved into the area, and sirens had wailed in the distance. He'd sat in his truck trying to collect himself and calm his heart as it battered against his chest. Frantically gulping air, he watched people swarm in awe around the site of the detonation. Hide in plain sight, he finally reasoned. Hide in plain sight and they wouldn't be able to tell him from the rest of the ogling spectators. He had gathered his courage, fortified it with more jolts from the pint, and headed back to the packed jumble of onlookers.

"Fool. Damned fool," he screamed as he raced down I-70 West. He'd walked swaggeringly into the trap that bitch had laid for him.

"I let her do it," he cried. He wept loudly, remembering how he'd been lounging against the Channel 20 Prime-Time van, giggling at the antics of the "live-action reporter." He had been congratulating himself for staying clear of the panning cameras as they gathered film for their stations. Then he saw her.

She was holding something tiny and metallic up to her face. He stared at her, wondering what she was up to. He had noticed her earlier but had discounted her as she wandered aimlessly, alighting here and there as a disoriented butterfly. He watched as she turned and aimed the silver sliver at him. Then the full realization of her actions hammered home in his brain.

"God damn. Good god, damn her!" he cried, turning the truck viciously.

She'd been holding a camera. She'd taken pictures of him. Nauseating fear had buckled his knees and rooted him to the spot. Her camera had clicked away as he turned to stone.

"She won't get away with it, I swear, she won't get away with it." He drove toward home screaming promises of revenge.

Chapter 13

"What the hell have you been doing all this time?" Captain Rhonn's face was a purple mask of high blood pressure. His screaming fairly rattled the windows in his office. Tru let his noise and fury flow over her without flinching.

"Have you had an opportunity to read my report?" she started to say. She kept her voice low, direct and unwavering. Her right hand gripped the arm of the chair to keep it from flying up and crashing across his mouth.

"I don't care about the damn report. I asked you a question. Another bomb goes off and what do I get? An investigation? A full report? Apprehension of the maniac that did it? No! All I get is you and Bob on television looking like some damn Mutt and Jeff team." Captain Rhonn collapsed in anger into his chair. He glared his exasperation at both Tru and Bob.

"The lab," Tru began, "has all the material we collected from the scene. I've talked with Haeres, the intended victim. I've secured a listing of all employees who worked with Reiling's janitorial service, the last two victims, and the names of anyone remotely related to all of them. The minute the hospital calls and tells me that the young woman who was injured has come around, I'm on my way to talk to her." Tru waved a hand at Bob, signaling for him to jump in and back her up.

"Right," Bob said. "We're waiting on the lab to give us something," he continued as he flipped through his notebook.

"Give you something! No one's going to give you a thing, idiot. I've got the chief, the commissioners, and half of city hall crawling down my neck. The media is having a field day, and the federal boys are pissing in their pants for a chance to give their expert advice and make us look like fools on every channel in town. No one's going to give you anything unless it's me, and that'll be my boot up your fat ass!"

"Captain?" Tru interrupted. "Captain, we do have some very decent leads. For one, the truck driver made deliveries all over town. According to Bill

Reiling, she had a habit of taking the mail and dropping it wherever she ran across a postal office. I think the bomber knew that and has been using her as his personal courier."

"You think so, do you?" Rhonn glared.

"Yes, I do. Whoever he is, he's there, around there, or working there. Close enough and familiar enough with the girl's routines to take advantage of them," Tru persisted.

"It will take a little time," Bob interjected.

"Shut up, Bob!" Rhonn yelled.

"He's right, Captain. There are fifteen companies in that industrial park. Any employee, past or present, day-worker, passerby, or person in the neighborhood could be our suspect," Tru defended.

"Then you haven't got shit."

"No, I think that's wrong," Tru dared, her voice firm and strong. "I believe we're closer than we've ever been. And I think we can get him."

"Get out of here. Both of you!" Rhonn said, slamming his hands down on top of his desk. "And don't come back until you can give me that guy wrapped up with a ribbon on his ass."

Bob scrambled out of his chair as quickly as his huge frame would allow. Tru let him have a clear path to the door. She followed him and muttered under her breath that the captain's blood pressure would push him into early retirement.

"Tru," Rhonn called to her.

"Yes?" she responded, composing her face as she turned to meet his eyes.

"Detective North. If you don't get this guy, if you drop the ball and anyone else gets hurt, I'll have your badge on my desk and your ass hitting the street at the same time. That's not a threat, that's a promise."

"I'm sure it is, Captain," Tru said, deciding her previous hope for the captain's early retirement had been too gracious.

Bob was standing anxiously outside the captain's door. She stopped to talk to him when she saw him raise an eyebrow at her.

"What are you going to do?" he asked.

"Everything I can, for one. I've got a lot of people to see and talk to, and plenty of things to check into. You go down and stick with the guys in the lab. See what they turn up. And try to stay out of the captain's way for a while. How's that sound to you?"

"Sounds like a plan."

"The only one I've got right now. We'll check with each other from time to time to keep us posted on developments." Tru patted the large man on his shoulder. "Don't let him get to you, Bob. He's an unmitigated asshole. You know your job, and we'll be fine."

"That's what we said about Brinkman, Sommers, and Younghons," Bob insisted.

"This time we'll be right," Tru said, trying to cheer herself and Bob. She knew he was worried about his family and the pension he was counting on. She didn't want to see the thirty-year veteran take a security job to make ends meet. She also didn't want to give the captain any more reason to scapegoat her.

Bob walked with her back to her cubicle where she retrieved her briefcase. She sorted through the papers then decided to go home and put the information on her computer.

"Call me at home if anything breaks. Okay?"

"Sure," Bob said as he sighed heavily and left the office. He walked despondently back down the hall toward the labs.

By late Wednesday evening, Tru had scanned all the documents she'd secured into her computer. It had taken her until ten o'clock to write the search-and-compile program she intended to run to cross check names, dates, agencies, and victims. Her mind felt like warm mush as she rechecked the program for errors and bugs. The telephone rang as she finished the third inspection.

"Hello?" she said softly into the phone.

"Tru?"

"Yes?"

"It's Marki, Tru. Are you okay? You don't sound like you," Marki said, puzzled.

"I've been working on something. Got a little lost and deep into it."

"I guess so. Do you always sound so distracted when you've been concentrating?"

"It's, it's, I don't know. You know, something about concentration and not being in the present. Maybe that's it."

"I see. Well, I called because I saw you on the news. You looked great, by the way," Marki said seductively. She had admired the way Tru responded coolly and confidently to the insistent probing from the reporters. Marki'd found herself beaming at Tru's image on the screen. She'd marveled at Tru's ability to appear so reserved on the surface. The TV image certainly wasn't the hungry Tru Marki recalled at their first meeting. The contrast was intriguing.

"Did I make you blush again?" Marki laughed.

"Not so you'd be able to tell from there," Tru laughed lightly.

"It's not too late. I could come over and we could see if I can do it in person?"

"I, I don't know. It is rather late," Tru faltered.

"Really? It's never too late to make you blush to your toes. Did you know that blushing is good for you?" Marki teased.

"I can't say that I did," Tru said, realizing where the conversation was headed.

"Yes, it is. It opens your pores, circulates your blood, and, warms you. The full-body blushes from a succulent climax are the best," Marki crooned.

"You're incorrigible." A ripple of desire raced through Tru. "Is this one of those lewd phone calls I've heard about?"

"Only if I can't convince you to let me come over and do it in person. Holding you would be wonderful. It could take hours."

Tru felt herself hesitating. Marki's suggestiveness worked on her and weakened her will. There was the memory of Marki's electrifying touch. The thought of being touched like that again crowded into her mind. She licked her lips and stood up to breathe deeper.

"Tru, you still there? I could be there in twenty minutes."

"Yes, I am," Tru said, resisting the rekindling of yearnings she'd submerged.

"Well then, why don't I come over?"

"I can't, it's too late. Besides, we have a date on Friday, don't we?"

"Yes, but that's not quite the same thing. Now is it?"

"You did say we were going to court. What you're suggesting doesn't exactly sound like courting." Tru wanted to deintensify the conversation.

"Courting has lots of definitions, my dear Detective Tru. Entice, tantalize, pursue, and seduce are a few."

"Friday night is only a day or so away. I think we can go slow. Don't you?"

"Have it your way. Fine by me, mostly," Marki said kindly. She knew she had touched a profound hunger in Tru. It aroused her. She would show a little patience in the pursuit. It would sweeten the taking.

"I'll see you Friday then."

"At eight sharp."

"Fine. Goodnight."

"Goodnight, Tru."

Tru set the receiver back in the phone's cradle and inhaled deeply to shake off the sensation that enveloped her. She had to get back to work. She turned, walked back to the computer, and sat in front of the monitor. A few minor adjustments, quick checks, and scans put the finishing touches on the program. Tru hit ENTER and turned off the glowing monitor.

"There. Now pulverize your little chips together and give me something to go on," she admonished the humming computer and headed for the bedroom. From his attentive napping repose on the couch Poupon watched her go.

Tru crawled into bed and fell into an exhausted sleep. Slowly her dreams merged into a confusion of Marki's persuasion, Rhonn's bellowing, and the sound of bombs thundering in the distance. Bodies pressed in on her from all sides. Her arms and hands shifted fitfully across her nakedness. She wrestled with bedcovers and threw them to the floor as her body was plundered by a woman's veiled hands. She arched and exclaimed in night's caress.

Chapter 14

They hadn't come for him. He still had some time to be safe. He could save himself. He had worried himself into a frenzy of packing and sorting through the things he wanted to take away with him. His tools, weapons, some clothes, and food consumed a large amount of the space in the camper he'd put on the bed of his truck. He didn't want to give them the opportunity to take him easily. He wanted time to wreak an exacting price.

By midnight he'd become calmer, more centered, and had struck upon the instrument of retaliation.

They would be helpless against him. Marie would have been proud.

"If you want it done right, you gotta do it yourself," he chanted as he cut the pages of the book. He'd found a hardback copy of *The Best of Yeats* by Ignatia Troy. It would be a poetic tool. The symmetry helped him concentrate and fix his mind to the tasks. It would be a surprise. The little bitch of a detective would never expect a thing. Dangerous literature? A gift from an admirer would arouse a little office curiosity but not one ounce of suspicion.

He smiled thinly as the blade of the scalpel traced the pocket and hollowed the book. Ten millimeters deep, fifty wide, and fifty long would give the space needed for the triggering device. Four ounces of plastique would separate her head from her body. If he were as lucky as he hoped, he might even get to take some of her police buddies with her.

He'd mail it tomorrow. A nice little overnight delight to greet her first thing Monday morning. He'd buy a protective bubble package from the baby bureaucrat at a postal counter. He'd chat with the clerk and let the stupid son of bitch put the stamps on it himself. Then he'd go buy a few beers, return home, and wait for the grisly news film in comfort.

He wanted no more mistakes. No slipups. He wasn't going to be anybody's fool again. He'd surprise the detective and create enough panic to let him slip away from his Missouri miseries.

"Come again another day," he sang as requiem to the detective.

Chapter 15

Tru awoke at six A.M. on Friday to the sound of the phone ringing noisily next to her head. Pulling herself up from the well of dreams, she grabbed the receiver.

"Yeah," she said groggily.

"Detective North?"

"Yes, who is it?"

"Detective North, this is Nurse Sapples at Troost General. I have a note here that says I'm supposed to call you when Carla Brighton wakes up," the lilting voice explained.

"She's awake then? Doing okay?" Stupid question, Tru chided herself. She rolled over and received a quick complaint from Poupon as her swinging foot accidentally tossed him to the floor.

"She's awake, stable, and improving. She's had a terrible shock, you know."

"Yes, I do know. What about her hearing? Can she hear?" Tru wondered sleepily how she would proceed with the questioning if Carla's ears were ruined. Writing, silly, she said to herself. I really need to have a cup of coffee before I try to talk to anyone.

"It's too early to know anything about permanent hearing loss. But she's responded to all the questions we've had. Of course, we've kept it pretty simple."

"Okay, I'll be there in about an hour. Let her know I'll be there."

"Sure thing, Detective."

Tru threw herself into the bathroom and took a quick, brisk, eye-opening shower. Towel drying her hair, she eyed herself in the mirror. One look told Tru that if she didn't style her hair, she would give poor Carla Brighton another undeserved shock.

Tru dressed in a pair of tan, lightly woven wool slacks, blue button-down cotton shirt, and black flats. Her favorite dark blue double-breasted jacket completed her attire. She looked in the mirror again and was somewhat relieved at the results.

"Poupon, Poupon, come out from wherever you are. Come stop sulking and get some breakfast," Tru called to the cat.

As she started toward the kitchen, she remembered the computer. It sat happily buzzing to itself on her desk.

"What have you got for me?" she asked and switched on the blank screen. She scrolled down the list of agencies and names of people. At the bottom of the twentieth page she found that the computer had generated some matches she was hoping to find.

Twenty names had been compiled as having had contact with one or more of the victims, galleries, and the organizations in the industrial park. Of those, four names showed up two or more times and matched across the fields of employees, clients, and companies: Jason Harding, Thomas Zoleberg, John Malory, and Clarence Berenger. It was a good concise list on which to work. She hoped her tinkering had generated real potential.

Tru glanced at her watch and knew it was still too early to call Bob Jones. He wouldn't be at the office until eight. She stuffed the list into the breast pocket of her jacket and dashed out the kitchen door to her car.

At the hospital Tru easily located Carla's room on the fifth floor. A security guard lounged inattentively near the door. A newspaper lay draped across his lap. Tru noticed a haggard, disheveled young woman sitting across from the guard.

"What are you doing here?" Tru asked the guard. He quickly came to full attention as she flashed her badge. The young woman in the chair seemed to brighten a little as Tru nodded to her.

"The family hired me. Rather, they hired my company to protect Ms. Brighton."

"Who are you?" Tru turned, and asked the young woman.

"I'm Martha Zweig, Carla's, Carla's friend," the young woman said haltingly.

"If you're a friend," Tru asked, "what are you doing out here, instead of being inside?"

Martha glanced bitterly at the guard. "Him. He won't let me in," she declared.

"Well," Tru said, turning back to the guard. "Why won't you let her inside?"

"Those're my orders. Ms. Brighton's father was very specific about keeping the press, the curious, and a certain Ms. Zweig away from his daughter. Just hospital, police, and family members. No so-called friends," he said, nodding in the direction of Martha Zweig.

Tru looked back at Martha and saw tears welling up in the young woman's eyes. "You are family, aren't you Martha?"

"Yes, ma'am. Her father didn't care a fart for her until this happened. She hadn't heard from him in over three months."

"Family like hell," the guard interjected. "Way I heard it, these two little queers have been shacked up like man and wife."

"That'll be enough out of you, ass wipe," Tru said as the anger rose from deep in her chest. "You sit there and keep that ugly mouth of yours closed or I'll report you to your agency for interfering in police business. You understand?"

The guard nodded in stunned silence.

"Come on, Martha. Let's go see how Carla's

doing," Tru said as she waved to Martha to follow her into the hospital room.

"Now, just a — " the guard began, and started to rise from his chair.

"What did I tell you?" Tru asked menacingly.

The guard sat back down and busied himself with rereading the newspaper. Tru escorted Martha into Carla's room. She didn't have time to close the door before cries of delight resounded from the young woman inside the room.

Tru stood self-consciously inside the closed door as she gave Carla and Martha a few moments together. Keeping her eyes averted, she tried not to indulge in a voyeurism of their concerned and passionate preoccupation with each other.

"Ms. Brighton," Tru said, finally interrupting the gleeful couple. "Ms. Brighton?"

"Oh, Carla, this wonderful woman made that bully let me come in. She's a cop!" Martha said excitedly.

"What?" Carla said, staring from Tru to Martha and back again.

"She's a cop," Martha said loudly and closer to Carla's ear.

"Oh," Carla smiled at Tru. "You have some questions?" She asked louder than necessary. Carla's ears rang with the clamor of injured eardrums and damaged follicles.

Tru nodded, took out her notepad, and walked to the bedside. She had decided that the strain of shouting would be too taxing on all concerned. She quickly wrote three questions and handed the notepad to Carla.

"No, I didn't see anyone near my truck before it blew up. Yes, we always have packages of one kind or another. And, no, I don't know anything about art, unless it has something to do with ancient meso-Americans," she answered and handed the pad back to Tru.

Tru pulled the list of computer generated names from her pocket and jotted a note to Carla.

"No, I don't think I know any of these people, except for the office staff. I never paid much attention to the guys who worked for Reiling's. Guys don't do anything for me," Carla said and beamed at Martha. "Why'd you help Martha?" Carla asked, turning back to Tru. Carla and Martha fixed their eyes on her.

Tru smiled at Martha and Carla. She retrieved the list, wrote quickly, tore the note off and handed it to Carla. Tru walked back to the door and waved good-bye to the young lovers.

"What's it say, Carla?" Martha asked as Tru walked out.

"Family, sweetie. It says, *Family*."

Arriving at the office, Tru fairly sprinted to the lab. She wanted to find out if they had discovered anything of importance she might use to help her narrow the list of suspects. The lab was housed in the three subbasement floors of the department. It managed to be even more drab and depressing than her own office environment. The lack of windows, the stale air, and the strange acidic aromas mixed noxiously. Tru practiced holding her breath as she searched for Bob Jones. She finally saw him coming out of the fingerprint examiners offices.

"What's up?" she called to him.

His head snapped up, and a look of surprise washed across his face. "You've got great timing, ole girl," he said glowingly.

"I warned you about that old stuff," she said as she met him in the hall. "What's this about timing?"

"Just this," Bob said, holding up a thin filmed paper. "Our boy may have finally gotten careless. This is his print, or rather, at least a very good partial. I'm going to fax it off to the FBI and have them run it through their computer."

"That's a gottcha," Tru said, patting Bob vigorously on the back. The large man barely seemed to notice. Tru imagined she'd probably hurt her hand before he'd notice her efforts.

"That's a you-got-him, Tru. This little partial came from that paper you found in the tire. If your luck holds out, we'll make this guy."

"Great!" Tru exclaimed. "I'm long overdue."

"Sure will disappoint the captain, though. He was counting on having both our butts for lunch." Bob smiled wryly at her.

"You just tell him he'll have to send out," Tru said in derision.

"Let's both tell him," Bob said as they headed back to their offices.

As they approached the captain's office they could see the short squared figure of the assistant police chief, Harold Baker, lowering himself into a chair. Rhonn saw them and anxiously waved them in.

"Are you two up to any good?" Rhonn barked.

"The best," Tru responded, and nodded cordially to the assistant chief. She handed Rhonn a copy of the partial fingerprint.

"That's it?" Rhonn asked narrowly.

"That's a partial. Bob's going to fax a copy to the FBI. If our guy has a record, been in the military, or received any security clearance, we've got him nailed," Tru explained.

"I know it's a partial, Detective. And in case you forgot, if the bomber isn't, doesn't, or hasn't been any of those things, you're still whistling in the wind." Rhonn kept his language and mannerism rigidly within department protocol for the assistant chief.

"While we're waiting to hear back from the FBI, I've got a few suspects. Bob and I can check up on them," Tru asserted.

"And just how did you come by those suspects?"

"I have a computer and scanner at home. I took the lists of victims, their clients, employees, and other names I collected, scanned them into the computer and wrote a cross-reference program," Tru said.

"Let me see it," Rhonn demanded.

Tru took the list out of her pocket and handed it over to the captain. The assistant police chief sat quietly and smiled at Tru. She hoped he was smiling because he liked her ingenuity but wondered if he just had gas.

"Since when do you know anything about computer programming?" Rhonn inquired.

"Since I started taking night classes two years ago. I finished my bachelor's long ago. But I've always been interested in how we might more effectively use the information we gather during investigations."

"You put together your own little program?" Rhonn asked crossly.

"Yes," Tru responded. She didn't like the tone Rhonn's voice was beginning to take.

"A couple of night classes and you think you're some kind of computer wizard. Is that the size of it?"

"No. I said I put the program together and ran the names through it. It generated some matches of people who have had contact with the victims or their places of work. It seems to me the bomber would have a reason, some connection to all —"

"It seems to you? It seems to you?" Rhonn's voice blustered.

"Captain, its something to go on. We don't have to wait for the FBI. I can find and talk to these . . ." Tru struggled to hold her temper in check.

"Get out of here. Take this pathetic list and get out of here. Try to look busy while we wait for the damn FBI to tell us who to arrest," Rhonn ordered.

Tru looked to the assistant chief of police and wondered if he'd speak. He never budged. Bob tapped her on the shoulder and motioned for her to follow him out of the office. Tru glared at Rhonn. He returned the glare and added a smirk.

"Of all the arrogant, misguided, sophomoric crap," Rhonn said as he followed them to the door and shut it.

Tru watched him turn back to the assistant chief. She could hear him mention her name several times before she was far enough away from the office to lose the sound of his voice.

"So much for luck," Bob offered.

"Yeah," Tru said. "All bad."

"What now?" he asked.

"I think you do the FBI, and I'll still do the list," Tru sighed. She wanted to go to the firing range and

174

put Rhonn's face on a target. She wanted to slowly pull the trigger and carefully shoot his ears, nose, eyes, and bobbing Adam's apple into little shreds of confetti. That's what she wanted to do. It would relax her. Make her feel better. But she wouldn't do it. She didn't have the time.

"Here," she said, going to the copy machine. "I'll start with the first ten and you go with the last ten. That gives you two of my top choices and I get two."

"Your top choices?"

"Yeah, they have more points of contact. At least, I think they do unless the captain's right about my programming. It was an experiment. But here's the idea. If one of these guys comes back belonging to that partial print, we're still going to win, whether the good Captain Rhonn likes it or not."

"You got it, Tru. I'd like to see him eat a little crow," Bob said.

"That is a take-out item, isn't it?" Tru winked at Bob and left the office. First on her list was a Clarence Berenger.

Chapter 16

"Great," Tru uttered aloud as she sat in her car looking at the Kansas City phone book. Four Berengers were listed. Two C. Berengers, one Clarence Berenger, and one C. "Bob" Berenger. Their addresses were spread across the confines of the metropolitan area.

"Could have been worse. He could have been a Smith," Tru told herself trying to recover hope. She sighed heavily and put the car in motion. She reached across to the computer console in her car and flipped on the switch. The monochrome screen came to life. Quickly she punched in the telephone book addresses and phone numbers of the Berengers living in the Kansas City metropolitan area and headed for a drive-thru restaurant.

The screen blanked and flashed its WORKING!! PLEASE WAIT! signal at Tru. She diverted her attention to the traffic and the audible growls coming from her stomach. She had missed breakfast in her hurry to the hospital. Tru snarled in irritation at the traffic as it slowed and delayed her hurry to find necessary nourishment.

As she turned into the lot holding the welcome sign of relief offered by the Burgers Galore fast-food drive-thru, a tiny metallic *ping* sound registered from the computer. Pulling up to the drive-thru speaker, Tru looked at the results of the first inquiries. The screen flashed the various Berengers' drivers license numbers and social security numbers as Tru told the Burgers Galore attendant that she wanted coffee, orange juice, and two egg fajitas to go. She typed her list of Berengers' identification information into a second inquiry mode.

Tru's order arrived, and she headed out across Main to a green park next to the plaza's giant bronze horse water fountain. She parked her car under the sweeping shade of a Blue Spruce and waited for the computer to disgorge its next response. She leaned back in her seat to enjoy the first bites of breakfast.

Moments later, as she sat washing down the first fajita with coffee, the computer scrolled a list for the matches of place, people, and profile of Berengers.

Carolyn Berenger	Female	African American	Age: 53
Catherine Berenger	Female	Caucasian	Age: 24
Clarence "Bob" Berenger	Male	Caucasian	Age: 72
Clarence L. Berenger	Male	Caucasian	Age: 36

Tru immediately discounted the women and concentrated her interest on the two men. Based on the profile she'd developed, Clarence Robert Berenger was too old. No known bombers had ever started their careers at that late age. The fires and passions of grievances, real or imagined, which still haunted a man in his twilight did not generally send them into murderous rages. Age would lend itself to patience and concentration of revenge but usually found other less violent methods to employ. At seventy-two, Clarence "Bob" Berenger would be more capable of the cunning and deceit of age than the direct engagement of youth. Tru imagined the older Berenger fighting in a court of law with the aid of hungry young attorneys, but not constructing bombs.

"Anything's possible," Tru reminded herself as she finished the orange juice. She took out a pen and jotted down the addresses of the two men. Noting their approximate locations on the map, she decided to see the older man first. He was closest. Clarence L. Berenger, Tru noticed, lived on Sin-A-Bar Road, over twenty miles from where she sat eating breakfast.

Taking out the one cigarette she allowed herself in the morning, Tru cleared the computer and ran Jason Harding's name. There was one Jason Harding. His address was on Swope Parkway. Tru looked back at the map. Harding's address was halfway to the younger Berenger's address. She figured that with a little luck she could make contact with all three men before the end of the day.

"Onward and upward, Mr. C. Bob," Tru said aloud as she turned her car back into the traffic flow and toward the home of Clarence "Bob" Berenger.

Chapter 17

By three o'clock in the afternoon, Tru was wondering if her luck was ever going to change for the better. As she drove toward the address on Sin-A-Bar, her mind whirled with the events of the last six hours.

She had spent more than an hour and-a-half with the old man, C. "Bob" Berenger. He'd been an interesting and obviously lonely old fellow. When she knocked on his door and identified herself, he all but pulled her into the house in his excitement. She endured long moments of impatience as he poured her a cup of coffee and told her about the loss of his wife and why he couldn't abandon the house that had been their home for over forty years.

She told him she was on police business and had asked to see the house. He was more than willing to provide her with a detailed examination, recounting the events and intrigues of the home. She was led from floor to floor and room to room. She tried to be patient. She focused her mind by looking for telltale signs of evidence as he bombarded her with the details of his life since retirement.

Afterward, Tru made a note to contact social services to find out if there was a way they could get him in contact with support groups to help alleviate the obvious loneliness and isolation of his life. When she finally got her chance to leave, she almost ran down the walkway back to her car.

Her computer had given her information that Jason Harding was thirty-one years old. A good age for a bomber. Before she arrived at his house, his social security number and information from the National Crime Information Center had told her that Jason Harding had served a hitch in the Army. He'd obtained expert marksmanship scores in weaponry, served in Operation Desert Storm as a demolition expert, and had received an undesignated medical discharge six months later. He was a near perfect fit to the profile she had developed. Tru radioed for backup before she arrived at the house. Close. Close only counted in horseshoes, hand grenades, and bomb blasts.

Tru and her backup surrounded the little house. Central headquarters had sent four patrol cars packed with officers, a bomb van lurking down the street, a flock of SWAT team members armed to the teeth, safety vests snugly fitted across every officer's chest, and a helicopter hovering over the scene.

Tru had used her car phone to call the house and firmly direct everyone inside to exit peacefully. She had to tell the frightened woman on the other end several times to put the phone down and exit the front door of the house. To everyone's surprise, and Tru's embarrassment, the two occupants quietly exited the home.

Mrs. Harding, Jason's mother, walked out onto the battered front porch, turned to look back inside, and waited for her son. He came out as quickly as he could, pushing and pulling the rubber-rimmed tires of his wheelchair with his one arm. Half of the SWAT team rushed them and whisked them from the porch as the other half entered the rear of the five-room house. There was nothing worth looking for. In the years since Desert Storm, Jason Harding had learned to take care of himself. But he could not have afforded, engineered, or attempted the physical manufacture of bombs. His injuries had been received in the service of his country, and he'd been returned to his mother with a tiny pension as thanks.

Several hours later, after extensive interviews, explanations, and apologies had been conveyed, Tru endured ten minutes of fiery conversation from Captain Rhonn. He'd blistered, fumed, and threatened her with a thirty-day suspension while assistant police chief Harold Baker had quietly looked on.

"Captain," Harold Baker finally interjected. "Captain, these things happen. It's not the time, but remind me to tell you the stink I once caused. It's a wonder I didn't get canned."

"What?" Rhonn said incredulously.

"Just this. The detective didn't cause any harm. Standard operating procedure was followed. We got a little excitement but no harm. We pay people to work, to dare, and to do. Sometimes it pays. Sometimes it doesn't. If we kicked everyone for daring, we would never catch the bad guys."

Tru stood mutely by and watched the exchange. She held her breath in amazement at the assistant chief's help and polished style.

"What are you suggesting?" Rhonn asked. There was hesitation in his voice.

"Simple. Get her out of here and back to work. You want to reprimand her? Fine. Put it in a letter of counseling and her personnel file. Then get on with it."

Rhonn's face purpled as the intention and direction of the orders from the assistant chief soaked in. He looked fleetingly at Tru and back to Baker.

"But . . . ?" Rhonn stumbled.

"No more and no less than you'd do to anyone else under the same circumstances. Mindful, of course, of her record of performance and years of service. Remember that from your supervision training lesson plans?" Baker persisted.

"Yes, sir," Rhonn replied.

"Good," Baker said, turning away from the captain and toward Tru. "Now, young lady, why don't you get back to work and try not to screw up for the next three months or so. Keep it clean and that letter of counseling will be removed. Fine with you?"

"Yes, sir," Tru said and turned on her heel to leave the captain's office. She didn't know what had happened. She was awash with surprise. Were there powers in the department or the universe she'd never suspected? Tru headed down the hallway to the parking lot and her car. She had one more name on the list of her best-guess suspects to check. She decided to start with him and do the less likely group tomorrow.

The sky had clouded up and was threatening cold rain by the time Tru left the station house. She couldn't keep her mind from wandering back to the strange and interesting encounter with Rhonn and the assistant chief of police. Shrugging to herself, she dashed between fat drops of rain as they began to dot and muddy the parking lot. Thunder peeled noisily overhead as a strong northerly wind whipped dirt, trash, and a last year's dead leaves against her feet.

"Another day in paradise," Tru said to the sky as she turned her vehicle onto the street.

Clarence Berenger, according to the information gleamed from the computer, NCIC, and internal records, was a caucasian male, thirty-six years old, widowed, and a member of the Missouri National Guard. He had served in Iran during and after Operation Desert Storm. His service operational job had been as a tank mechanic. He wasn't the nice profile fit that Jason Harding had been. Not even close. And Harding's nice fit had blown up in her face.

Her eyes narrowed on his name. She wasn't going to make the same mistake twice. There would be no backup. He was another widower. She wondered how long it would take her to get out of his house if he was as chatty as old C. Bob had been.

The clouds rushed and swirled above her as she

drove down and off Swope Parkway onto Sin-A-Bar road. The threatening cloudbursts arrived as she drove along the roadway. Bumping along, Tru surmised that the county maintenance department had put the Sin-A-Bar on a do-last memo. Potholes, shattered asphalt, and the obscuring rains forced Tru to slow her vehicle in order to dodge the surface treacheries. As she drove, Tru could see gravel and dirt driveways heralded by the placement of roadside mailboxes. The drives meandered off the main roadway and back to sharply rising mounds of tree-sheltered lots.

Tru squinted at the names on the mailboxes and tried to find the name Berenger on one of them. Three miles later she came to the end of Sin-A-Bar as it coursed back up and onto Highway 71.

"Shit," she said in frustration. It either wasn't there or she'd missed it. The rain was coming harder. She backed her car up and turned around on the soft edges of the road. As she drove back down Sin-A-Bar she turned on the car's defroster to clear the condensation from the inside of the windshield.

"One forty-nine sixty-five Sin-A-Bar. Berenger's supposed to be at one forty-nine sixty," Tru muttered to herself as she passed a brightly painted mailbox stand. She slowed the car at the second driveway. There was no name on it. The numbers had become smeared and worn to unintelligibility. Tru rolled down her window and stared up the driveway. A house lay darkened at the top. Wind-driven rain beat across her face as she glimpsed a lone figure walking down the drive toward her. She rolled the window up and waited.

Tru watched the man reach the mailbox, open it,

and pull out what appeared to be a stack of bills and fliers. He stood in the downpour, then glanced up as he became aware of Tru's car sitting motionless on the opposite side of the road.

Tru waved to him nonchalantly and drove her car into his driveway. She stopped alongside him. He waited, letting the rain wash over her as she rolled her window down.

"Hi. I'm lost. Do you know where a Clarence Berenger lives?" As she watched, his eyes grew round and his mouth fell open.

"Arrgh!" He screamed at her and fell back, clambered to his feet, and sprinted up the drive toward the house.

"Wait!" Tru yelled as she gunned the car up the driveway. The rainwashed gravel and dirt made the driveway a slick clay-and-mud-filled stream. Tru's car fishtailed and bounced toward the trenches on either side. She'd given it too much gas for the surface conditions and struggled frantically with the steering. She worked furiously to keep the car from heading toward the churning ditches. The slimy mud betrayed her. The car dropped and crashed into the wide U-shaped trough as Tru grabbed the radio microphone. She yelled her location and need for backup. Throwing the mike down on the seat, she pushed the car door open. As she scrambled out of the car, she pulled her gun and ran after the man.

She sloshed up through the churning mud of the driveway. "Mr. Berenger!" Tru yelled as she gained the front porch. Under the wide protective cover of the porch roof, Tru pounded on the door and flattened herself against the house. "Mr. Berenger!" she called.

Shots rang out as two gaping holes appeared inches from where her chest and head lay against the door jamb. At the sound of the blasts, Tru propelled herself off the porch and into the wet grass and mud. Another blast sprang the hinges while she scrambled under the steps.

"Bitch!" Berenger screamed at Tru through the ruined door. Three more shotgun blasts punctuated and scored the rolling, rocking thunder of the afternoon. He followed the shots and bounded out onto the splattered porch.

Mud and rain washed stingingly into Tru's eyes as she rolled herself underneath the porch for protection. She raised her gun and fired three rounds rapidly at the point where she thought she'd heard his foot stop.

A bloodcurdling scream broke over Tru's head and suggested that one of her bullets had found its mark. The scream was immediately followed by a shotgun blast that pierced the porch floor. It sent shatters of splintering wood and pellets grazing into her left shoulder. Tru gasped in pain and rolled away. He fired again. This time he missed her.

She crawled crablike and shoved herself backward under the porch, away from certain death. Tru twisted and fired four times in rapid succession. She dragged herself backwards. Her body jolted against the house and she reeled away, struggling to escape the entrapment.

As she wiped the rain from her eyes, Tru saw the

edge of the porch, the rain beyond and heard the crack of lightning split the air. Dread, desperation, and recklessness mixed wildly in her. She raised up and tried to lurch through the opening only to feel the bone-crunching slam of her back as it struck the supporting cross beams. She could hear him reloading the shotgun as he staggered above her. Firmly grasping the semiautomatic, she bunched her legs and scrambled furiously. She flung herself out into the yard and into the open. She lunged and rolled onto her back. Blinking through the rain, she searched upward for her assailant.

The indistinct impression of a man staggering under the protective roof swam in her eyes. The ominous sound of a shotgun shell cracking into the chamber caused her lips to peel back in a desperate grinning contortion. She rolled and fired at Berenger.

Her panicked confrontation caused him to jerk his shotgun wide as he ducked for cover. Her bullet barely missed him as he flung himself back inside the house.

Staggering to her feet, her wounded shoulder viciously stinging, Tru moaned. Crouching, she ran toward the house and took anxious cover against its peeling paint.

Tru swiveled her head. She looked to the windows above her, to the far end of the house, and back to the front porch again. Rain pounded and the crashing of thunder prevented her from hearing movement within the structure. Ducking below the windows, she ran to the rear of the house. She got there in time to see the camper-laden truck careening wildly. It crashed backward into the detached garage, stalled, and uselessly spun its wheels in reverse.

Tru couldn't see the driver but knew it was Berenger. She raised her weapon and fired once into the windshield. Her bullet hit and shattered the middle of the rain-splattered glass.

Berenger smashed the gears into drive. The truck reared forward and roared down the driveway. Tru ran falteringly around the house and fired at the receding truck.

She grabbed a second clip of rounds on her belt. With a smooth release the empty dropped out of the weapon as she slammed home the full clip. Tru aimed at the driver's side compartment and emptied all fourteen rounds into the soft tin of the camper.

The truck lurched, braked, slid wildly in the clay mud, and slammed into Tru's car near the end of the driveway. The truck's motor roared and its tires spun ineffectually against her ruined vehicle. No one got out of the cab.

Tru wobbled uncertainly toward the truck. She reached for the last clip at her waist, let the empty drop at her feet, and cautiously approached the silent truck. The rain battered her as the wailing of distant sirens reached her through the downpour.

As Tru approached the camper, an explosion ripped through the cab of the truck. It was instantaneously followed by a twin eruption from the camper. Fire, flash, heat, and concussions propelled themselves toward her.

Tru was thrown backward and sprawling into the muddy gravel. She lay outstretched, and the cold sharp rocks dug against her back. She was dazed. She barely heard the thunder rumbling over her head and the wail of sirens that seemed to grow distressingly distant.

In the last moments of consciousness, she realized she wouldn't be able to keep her promised dinner date with Marki.

Chapter 18

"Are you up to visitors?"

"Hrrumphh," Tru struggled to make her throat and mouth work together.

"Are you up to visitors?" the detached voice persisted.

"Yes ... no ..." Tru responded. The pain in her shoulder and the throbbing of her head made her want to retreat to protective sleep.

"Tru? Tru, are you there?"

"No," she protested.

"Come on now, Tru." The voice demanded her attention.

Tru opened her eyes, and the wavering image of an auburn-haired woman slowly shimmered before her. She blinked, closed her eyes, and willed a clearer focus. She opened her eyes again, and Marki's face grew distinct.

"Wha ..." Tru labored to make her tongue cooperate.

"Me. It's me," Marki urged.

"Yes," Tru said, feeling the hand that held hers and squeezing it to signal recognition.

"You're quite the character. Do you know that?" Marki said, trying not to let her distress creep into her voice.

"Oh," Tru managed. She was feeling more awake but not cognizant as to place or time.

"Yes, you are. For a bit of a thing, you certainly can get into quite a mess. You've had everyone worried. I've put my credentials on the line just to get in here to see you."

"How's that?" Tru managed.

"I told them I'm your — what do you call it? ... your shrink. It's on the hospital records. How am I going to seduce you with that hanging over my head?"

"Very carefully?" Tru offered.

"No doubt," Marki mused. "No doubt."

Tru tried to smile, but medications sent her smile awry as sleep claimed her again.

* * * * *

Bob Jones was the first to see Tru walk into the office. A huge grin spread over his face. She'd been in the hospital for five days. He was glad to see her and moved toward her with more speed than people would ever have suspected him capable.

Tru looked up to see him charging down the narrow cubicle pathway. She braced herself. He arrived in front of her and, with all the gentleness and civility he had at his command, gingerly reached out to lay a welcoming hand on her unwounded shoulder.

"How ya doin' ole girl?"

"Bob," Tru raised her eyes to the imposing man, "does your wife know about our impending engagement?" Tru asked.

"No, but for you, I'll break it to her gently." He laughed and led her towards the unit.

During the next twenty minutes Tru was awash in a sea of friends, coworkers, and well-wishers. It felt good. It felt like the camaraderie they'd shared before Captain Rhonn. They were kind, not overly solicitous, mocking her, derisive about the extent of her injuries. It was good. They were caring and interested in their own clumsy way. She was relaxed, accepting, and comfortable in their cavalier behavior. Coming home to their bantering was as it should be. She liked the men and women who served with her. They might not be understood or appreciated, but they were part of the family she'd chosen.

Bob noticed when Tru's eyes fell on the captain's door.

"He's away for a while," Bob said grinning.

"You're kidding?"

"No. Some little sabbatical or other. Seems as though they sent him out to learn a few things about advanced supervision. Can you imagine? All that talent and he's been sent for a refresher?" Bob beamed maliciously.

"Well," Tru said, "couldn't have happened to a nicer guy." She smiled broadly at Bob and even more at the ten-foot hoagy they hauled out to devour.

"Always a good reason for stuffing our faces," Tru said amused.

They ate, talked, and laughed through the major part of the morning. While they enjoyed the morning's "Welcome Back," Bob Jones explained to Tru the information they had been able to glean from Clarence Berenger's house.

"Berenger was apparently avenging his wife's death. We found a small notebook he started to keep after she died. She'd been working long hours for Southwick. No hanky-panky, or anything like that. She'd gotten a late start home and simply went to sleep at the wheel. Died instantly when she hit a bridge abutment. Berenger blamed Southwick. We can only guess that his grief became the focus in his life and he blamed all art types. We found several copies of the K.C. *Entrepreneur Magazine* in the house. Each victim had appeared in the magazine a month or so before he sent them a bomb."

"But why the Olathe guy first?" Tru asked.

"Who knows. Practice maybe. He got better didn't he? Southwick died. He made his own little boxes. A real craftsman. He apparently sold some of them in a few of the art shops before his wife died. Music boxes mostly. There are people in town who own one of those things and don't know their connection. Ironic isn't it?"

"If you say so. Though it's not my definition of irony," Tru said, shaking her head.

Bob walked Tru back to her desk. He asked how long she was supposed to be in on a first day back.

"Until I get too tired to be here," she responded.

"Since I'm senior man, I say it's time you headed home." He guided her into her cubicle. "Why don't you take your toys and get out of here?"

Looking into the cubicle, Tru saw the roses, cards, and package sitting on her desk. She smiled and looked wonderingly up at Bob.

"Not me ole girl. My wife would kill me," he said determinedly. "I haven't sent her flowers and candy since we were in our twenties — or before."

Tru removed the card from the flowers and read it.

True to you is only one desire. It was signed "M. C." Tru blushed. She hadn't seen Marki since she'd been released from the hospital.

"M. C.," Bob read over her shoulder. "Is there anything we need to talk about here?" he asked, using his best authoritarian voice.

"Not a thing. Not a thing you would ever need to know about, Bob. I assure you," Tru responded as she picked up the flowers, cards, and box. "I think I'll take your advice and call it a day. Besides, it looks as though I need to make a little thank-you call. Think you can do without me?"

"We'll manage. Somehow."

"See you later." Tru waved as she left the office. There was someone she wanted to talk to. She hurried to her car and lovingly put her gifts on the seat next to her.

Walking into her apartment, Tru set the flowers and package on the dining table. She went to the bathroom and luxuriated in a long bath awash with scented soaps. The phone rang. Scrambling out of the tub, Tru discovered she'd missed the call. But the recorder had captured the message.

Marki, according to Sara, would be at home in a little more than twenty minutes.

Tru hurried into her clothes, grabbed up the package and ran out to her car. It was everything she could do to keep from stopping the car to open the package and see what Marki had sent her.

"There you are," Marki said brightly as Tru walked into her house.

"And there you are," Tru smiled broadly. "Your secretary said you left early and I could find you here." Tru carried the package under her left arm.

"Great secretaries are hard to come by. I'm glad she told you. What do you have there?" Marki asked as she took Tru by the hand and led her into the living room.

"The gift you sent," Tru said as she placed the package on the coffee table.

"I sent you flowers, dear. Not candy. Who else do you have on a string?"

"No one. Really."

"The evidence," Marki said, "would seem to contradict you."

"No, really. You didn't send it?" Tru picked up the package and looked at the postmark. It was dated last Friday. There was no return address.

"Then who —" Marki started to ask and stopped when she saw the look on Tru's face. "What is it?"

"When did you send the flowers?"

"Just this morning. You told me you intended to go back to work. I thought it would be a nice surprise."

"This package has been sitting on my desk since Monday or Tuesday at the latest."

"Is that an odd thing?"

Tru gingerly set the package on the coffee table. Streaks of electricity ran through her scalp as she recognized the scrawled cursive style of the handwritten address.

"Too odd to discount. I need to make a phone call, then I think we should go over to my place," Tru urged.

"Would being in your territory make you feel safer?" Marki asked, dropping her voice half an octave.

"Safer than being here right now," Tru said as she turned to find a phone.

"Whatever suits your fancy. But I don't think it will be as safe as you might imagine."

"You think not?" Tru smiled as she rapidly punched the number for the bomb squad.

While Marki went to get a coat, Tru talked rapidly into the phone. She gave them the address and assured them the house was being evacuated. They promised to take care of the details. Tru told them she'd leave a door unlocked for them. She would have a lot of explaining to do to Marki, but that could wait. She hoped Marki would understand.

"Ready when you are, Tru," Marki said as she returned from her room. She placed her hands on Tru's hips, pulled her close, and took her into a deep sweet kiss.

"Well," Tru said as she came up for air, "maybe my place isn't going to be very safe at all."

"Not from me. Not now or at least not very safe for long," Marki said as they turned to leave.

COURTED by Celia Cohen. 160 pp. Sparkling romantic
encounter.   ISBN 1-56280-166-X $11.95

SEASONS OF THE HEART by Jackie Calhoun. 240 pp. Romance
through the years.   ISBN 1-56280-167-8   11.95

K. C. BOMBER by Janet McClellan. 208 pp. 1st Tru North
mystery.   ISBN 1-56280-157-0   11.95

LAST RITES by Tracey Richardson. 192 pp. 1st Stevie Houston
mystery.   ISBN 1-56280-164-3   11.95

EMBRACE IN MOTION by Karin Kallmaker. 256 pp. A whirlwind
love affair.   ISBN 1-56280-165-1   11.95

HOT CHECK by Peggy J. Herring. 192 pp. Will workaholic Alice
fall for guitarist Ricky?   ISBN 1-56280-163-5   11.95

OLD TIES by Saxon Bennett. 176 pp. Can Cleo surrender to a
passionate new love?   ISBN 1-56280-159-7   11.95

LOVE ON THE LINE by Laura DeHart Young. 176 pp. Will Stef win Kay's
heart?   ISBN 1-56280-162-7 $11.95

DEVIL'S LEG CROSSING by Kaye Davis. 192 pp. 1st Maris Middleton
mystery.   ISBN 1-56280-158-9   11.95

COSTA BRAVA by Marta Balletbo Coll. 144 pp. Read the book,
see the movie!   ISBN 1-56280-153-8   11.95

MEETING MAGDALENE & OTHER STORIES by
Marilyn Freeman. 144 pp. Read the book, see the movie!
                                          ISBN 1-56280-170-8   11.95

SECOND FIDDLE by Kate Calloway. 208 pp. P.I. Cassidy James'
second case.   ISBN 1-56280-169-6   11.95

LAUREL by Isabel Miller. 128 pp. By the author of the beloved
Patience and Sarah.   ISBN 1-56280-146-5   10.95

LOVE OR MONEY by Jackie Calhoun. 240 pp. The romance of
real life.   ISBN 1-56280-147-3   10.95

SMOKE AND MIRRORS by Pat Welch. 224 pp. 5th Helen Black
Mystery. ISBN 1-56280-143-0   10.95

DANCING IN THE DARK edited by Barbara Grier & Christine
Cassidy. 272 pp. Erotic love stories by Naiad Press authors.
ISBN 1-56280-144-9   14.95

TIME AND TIME AGAIN by Catherine Ennis. 176 pp. Passionate
love affair. ISBN 1-56280-145-7   10.95

PAXTON COURT by Diane Salvatore. 256 pp. Erotic and wickedly
funny contemporary tale about the business of learning to live
together. ISBN 1-56280-114-7   10.95

INNER CIRCLE by Claire McNab. 208 pp. 8th Carol Ashton
Mystery. ISBN 1-56280-135-X   10.95

LESBIAN SEX: AN ORAL HISTORY by Susan Johnson.
240 pp. Need we say more? ISBN 1-56280-142-2   14.95

BABY, IT'S COLD by Jaye Maiman. 256 pp. 5th Robin Miller
Mystery. ISBN 1-56280-141-4   19.95

WILD THINGS by Karin Kallmaker. 240 pp. By the undisputed
mistress of lesbian romance. ISBN 1-56280-139-2   10.95

THE GIRL NEXT DOOR by Mindy Kaplan. 208 pp. Just what
you'd expect. ISBN 1-56280-140-6   11.95

NOW AND THEN by Penny Hayes. 240 pp. Romance on the
westward journey. ISBN 1-56280-121-X   11.95

HEART ON FIRE by Diana Simmonds. 176 pp. The romantic and
erotic rival of *Curious Wine*. ISBN 1-56280-152-X   11.95

DEATH AT LAVENDER BAY by Lauren Wright Douglas. 208 pp.
1st Allison O'Neil Mystery. ISBN 1-56280-085-X   11.95

YES I SAID YES I WILL by Judith McDaniel. 272 pp. Hot
romance by famous author. ISBN 1-56280-138-4   11.95

FORBIDDEN FIRES by Margaret C. Anderson. Edited by Mathilda
Hills. 176 pp. Famous author's "unpublished" Lesbian romance.
ISBN 1-56280-123-6   21.95

SIDE TRACKS by Teresa Stores. 160 pp. Gender-bending
Lesbians on the road. ISBN 1-56280-122-8   10.95

HOODED MURDER by Annette Van Dyke. 176 pp. 1st Jessie
Batelle Mystery. ISBN 1-56280-134-1   10.95

These are just a few of the many Naiad Press titles — we are the oldest and
largest lesbian/feminist publishing company in the world. We also offer an
enormous selection of lesbian video products. Please request a complete
catalog. We offer personal service; we encourage and welcome direct mail
orders from individuals who have limited access to bookstores carrying our
publications.